Y0-BEP-056

Let's mark the true adv... is within

Connie B

"*Sydney Knight is a delightfully compelling character.
Her strengths and vulnerabilities
are masterfully combined and
visually illustrated. Her relationships are
both exciting and heart-wrenching,
from her marriage to Mac
to her experiences with Doctor Drew.*"
- Molly E. Smith - literary agent -

"*I felt like I was in the jungle with these characters
experiencing their adventures and their passion.
Well written, filled with a bonus of
Amazonian and shamanic insights.*"
- Yatra Review -

"*A novel with depth and style.
Empowering, romantic, adventurous.
It's all there. First love. Broken hearts.
Second chances.*"
- 11:11 Studios -

"JUNGLE MOON" is the first in a series
of Sydney Knight adventure/romance novels
by Connie Bickman
Travel with Sydney
through Australia, Africa, Russia, Ecuador,
and other international destinations
in upcoming romance/adventure novels.

Also available by Connie Bickman

"THE TOUCHSTONE DIARY" series
Book I "The Red Thread"
and Book II "Bloodlines and Promises,"
(both books in one volume - book three is in progress)
*"Well researched with detailed and pleasantly shocking
revelations of an alternative Jesus/Mary Magdalen story.
Bickman brings us through life, death and the afterlife...a fresh
view of the original foundation of spirituality."* Kathryn Harwig
ISBN 9780991171309

**"TRIBE OF WOMEN - A Photojournalist Chronicles
the Lives of Her Sisters Around the Globe"**
*"Connie Bickman is a gifted author. She delivers uplifting
messages that empower and open the hearts of women and
men of all ages, cultures, and backgrounds."* Doreen Virtue
published by New World Library
ISBN 1-57731-130-2

JUNGLE
MOON

Connie Bickman

Although the Amazon Jungle Lodge setting in this book is an actual place, "Jungle Moon" is a work of fiction. Names, (with the exception of some Amazonia Expedition management), and characters are the product of the author's imagination or are used fictitiously. Some instances may relate to the author's personal experiences and local traditions, however resemblances to actual events and/or persons living or deceased is pure coincidence.

Copyright 2016 Connie Bickman
Yatra Publications. All rights reserved.

Grateful acknowledgement is made to
Paul and Dolly Beaver
of Amazonia Expeditions, Tampa, Florida/Iquitos, Peru
www.perujungle.com

Printed in the United States of America
ISBN-13: 978-1530520336
ISBN-10: 1530520339

"A wound is the place where light enters you."
Rumi

CHAPTERS

Jungle Moon ~ 8 ~ Connie Bickman

~ one ~

SHATTERED DREAMS

The monotonous drone of 747 should have lulled her to sleep. She was exhausted.

Sydney's writing assignment in Africa had logistically been grueling. She thrived on adventure, but after weeks of traveling from country to country while documenting cultural diversity within local tribes, she was glad to be heading back to New York. She propped her pillow against the oval window, flipped up the armrests and stretched out across all three seats, grateful to have the row to herself. She turned off the overhead light and movie monitor. The scene across from her in seats 13B and C was better than any of the movies the plane's tiny TV screen could provide.

"They must be on their honeymoon," Sydney thought. The young couple couldn't keep their hands off each other. They didn't seem to care that they were in plain sight, or that those around them could hear their muffled moans as kisses of passion engulfed their senses. The strap on the girl's tank top fell off her shoulder and for a moment it looked as if her lover was going to undress her completely. She quickly grabbed the airline blanket from the empty seat next to her and covered them both. It didn't take much to imagine what was going on beneath the blanket as their hands roamed and their bodies moved to each other's urges.

They weren't the only ones feeling the heat in their loins. "I shouldn't be watching this," Sydney reprimanded herself as she squirmed in her seat, recalling the flame of ignited lust. Soon a flight attendant stopped at row 13 and asked if there was anything she could get for the couple. A male voice from 14C said, "Get them a room," which brought a chuckle from other passengers who either enjoyed or were embarrassed by the scene. The young couple sat up and clumsily adjusted the blanket, looking around as if they suddenly realized they weren't in the honeymoon suite. The attendant expertly reached over, turned on the overhead light and flipped down their tray, placing two glasses of water before them.

"Newlyweds?" she smiled.

Sydney reached for the romance novel she had packed in her bag. There was no hope of sleep now.

~~~~~~

Sydney Knight was used to adventure. She began her career working at newspapers and went on to become an international photojournalist, traveling the world to document native cultures, traditions and environmental issues. Most people thought it was a glamorous job, but it was hard work. There were long days of travel, short stays in hotel after hotel, early mornings, late nights, and a lot of stressful deadlines. Regardless of the rigorous schedules, travel, writing, and photography had became Sydney's passion. It was also her escape.

As successful as Sydney was in her professional life, it was the opposite when it came to romance. A marriage that began happily at age nineteen, failed miserably as the years progressed.

Sydney had been divorced from her high school sweetheart for years. She knew her inability to find the right man in her life had a lot to do with her marriage. Mac had been a good husband in many ways. He was handsome, a great provider, and could fix anything. He was a good man. But there were things missing in the relationship. Sydney overlooked it at first. She was young and had accepted Mac's inability to show emotion, to touch, hug, even to say he loved her.

"Of course I do, I'm still here, aren't I?" he would say, when she asked why he never told her he loved her. She understood and accepted it because his parents weren't "touchers" either. Mac didn't grow up in the loving atmosphere she had. Her parents were always holding hands, sitting next to each other on the couch and having real conversations. In all the years of her and Mac's marriage, plus their courtship, she had only seen his parents kiss once, and that was on their 40th wedding anniversary, because guests at the dinner were striking their champagne glasses, a request for the couple to kiss. When Sydney would try to give Mac a kiss or hug, just because she felt like it, he'd push her away and tell her not to hang on him. Touching was reserved for sex. Mac had been a good lover once the door was closed behind them, but things seemed to change through the years. The sensuous passion that began their sex life had now given way, most of the time, to slam-bam-thank-you-mam.

Mac was an engineer and he worked hard. He came home tired. Sydney was a romantic. She wanted the magic, the feelings that sent tingles down her back when he ran his hands over her body. She wanted to make love. Not just have sex.

"I don't think he really likes me," Sydney remembered telling a friend.

"Of course he does," her friend responded. "He loves you."

But Sydney knew there was a difference between like and love. Mac was a workaholic—but he also drank too much, partied too much with his buddies and occasionally with other women. . .she knew, but still, she contended he was a good man. She loved him. She just couldn't tolerate his indiscretion anymore—especially time spent with a married girlfriend of hers. She had asked them both about their relationship and they told her they were just friends. They were just talking. Talking! Mac was the silent type who rarely spoke unless he had something important to say. What did he have to say to Janet that he couldn't talk with her about? She was his wife. Sydney finally point blank asked Mac if they were having an affair. He said he had never had sex with Janet. Sydney told him there were many other ways to have an affair. He scoffed at her and left the room, putting the blame on her—as if she was the guilty one for accusing him. How stupid did he think she was?

Sydney remembered their last anniversary. They had a few friends over, couples they had known for years. Janet and her husband, Jeff, were among their circle of friends and it would have been awkward not to invite them. Sydney had purposely chosen a very romantic and suggestive card for Mac. She signed:

"To Mac, my high school sweetheart and my devoted, loving husband. You are my forever love. Sydney"

He smiled as he read it. She wasn't sure if it was because he felt the same, or because he was a little nervous. She wanted to put a condom inside the envelope as a clue that she knew about him and Janet, but decided that might be inappropriate in front of their friends. Instead she folded tickets for Mexico inside the card. They had talked about a vacation for months, or maybe it was just her that had brought it up each time. She knew it would never happen unless she took the reins. She even thought maybe it might revive their relationship. Sydney gave Mac a big hug and a suggestive kiss when he commented on the tickets.

"I love you, honey," she gushed, as their friends clapped and joked about going with them. She was surprised that Mac didn't push her away or object. Of course, he wouldn't push her away in front of their friends. Sydney took pleasure in watching Janet's reaction to this public display of affection. She stared directly at Janet, hoping it would send a message to lay off her husband. That's as much as Sydney could handle as far as confrontation. Conflict made her weak. Years later she wished she had had it out with Janet. Maybe things would have been different. Then again, maybe not.

Their vacation in Cancun had been promising. Mac was a completely different person away from home and they actually had a great time together. They made love like they did when they were young, exploring each other's bodies and fulfilling each other again and again, as if they were just discovering their passion. They flirted underwater as they snorkeled the coral reefs and made love in the moonlight on a sandy deserted beach. They drank shots of tequila with other tourists and danced on the tables in a seaside bar, so out of character for Mac. He bought her a necklace from a Mexican woman on the beach, placing it around her neck like a new wedding gift, while his lips caressed her shoulders under the starry skies. It was all very romantic. There were no other distractions. She didn't know he could be like this, so attentive, so loving. It's what she had wanted from Mac all along —simple moments to show that he loved her.

Sydney had renewed hopes for their marriage— until they returned home and their relationship soon fell into the same rut as before. Back to work. Back to everyday living. Back to that unexpressive space that distanced them. She asked Mac what had gone wrong, reminding him how romantic and alive they were in Cancun. Now they were back to an almost nonexistent relationship. Mac just shrugged his shoulders.

"What do you mean?" he said. "That was vacation. This is life."

"So, we have to go on vacation for you to love me?"

He quickly replied. "I enjoyed our time in Cancun, but we're not in Mexico any more. We're home and things are different here. I work hard. You have everything you need and want—this house, your car, your job, clothes, all your hobby stuff. We have responsibilities and jobs to do. Grow up Sydney. This is life."

That stung. Did he really think this was the way married couples should act? Was the example of his parent's lackluster relationship that engrained into him? To him the vacation was just a wild fling and now they were back to reality. Working hard and making money were his goals in life, not having a loving, fulfilling relationship.

Months later, when Sydney finally told Mac she wanted a divorce, she just couldn't do this anymore, he was remorseful and said he didn't want her to leave. He was so attentive to her for a few days that she had hopes for them. Maybe the thought of losing her rekindled his feelings. But, Sydney soon realized that, of course, Mac wanted her to stay. She was his housekeeper, his mother, his bookkeeper, his safety net. She took care of him.

It hit her hard one day when she unexpectedly came home early from work and found him in bed, their bed. . .with Janet.

Sydney was discreet. When she saw Janet's car in the driveway she reluctantly walked around the house and looked in the windows. Not seeing anyone in the living room or kitchen, her heart sank as she slowly walked around to their bedroom window. She saw them there, through the glass. She didn't want to watch, but couldn't believe what she was seeing. With their naked bodies pressed together, Mac lowered Janet to the bed as his hands fondled her breasts and his lips followed. Janet arched her back in response to his touch and soon they were moving together, in rhythm to each other's passions. Mac was caressing Janet the way he used to make love to *her*. He was giving this other woman what *she* had longed for, what *she* was denied. How could this be happening? Was she that bad of a lover? How could she have been so naive? Sydney wanted to bang her fists against the window and scream. She wanted to throw a rock through the glass and pull their sweaty bodies apart or hose them off like dogs in heat. Through her anger came tears of deception, of a dreaded realization that this most likely had happened before. Sydney turned and quickly walked away. It would have been too messy to walk in on them, too emotional. She didn't like confrontation.

Those were the scars Sydney brought into a relationship. She would never allow herself to be vulnerable again, to set herself up for deceit. It was a trust issue she didn't want to deal with. At the same time, she knew that in order to move on she would some day have to deal with this old wound, this deep, dark gash that sliced open her heart so long ago. Meditation, visualizing cutting the etherial cords that connected them, therapy—nothing worked. Mac had been her first love—since she was 15-years-old. They grew up together. She reached deep inside herself and had somehow forgiven him. That's how strong her love was. Yet, even though she still loved him, she was glad they were no longer married. Her feelings were more sisterly now. It was easier. Somehow they had remained friends—even after he and Janet married.

~~~~~

After the divorce, Sydney quit her job at the newspaper and moved to New York. She got a job as a photojournalist and threw herself into her work.

She made a list of what she wanted in her life. What *she* wanted. Progressively she worked to check off and satisfy those goals. She had gotten to the point where she was happy with the woman she had become. The woman she had carved out of a stone cold love. She had set her expectations high if she were ever to become serious about a man again. She wouldn't settle for less. Sydney had friends and dated socially, but after a few disappointing relationships she took more work assignment to keep herself busy. She masked her emotions and fulfilled her life through the lens of her camera and in the pages of words she wrote for documentaries and magazines.

But as the years passed, Sydney was slowing down. As much as she loved traveling and working, she was feeling the need for something more in her life again. She was tired of being alone. She had made a good living in her career and didn't need the money, so was being more selective about her assignments. She was looking for love these days, not adventure. But old habits are hard to break. In Sydney's case, those old habits seemed to coincide with her poor choice of partners.

~ two ~

TRIAL AND ERROR

Sydney met Richard at a party. He was a rich investment banker, suave and handsome. He immediately gravitated toward her. She was not the tall, thin, model type he usually dated, but she was strikingly beautiful with an air of confidence that intrigued him. She was about 5'6" with rounder features, stark blue eyes and long blonde hair braided down her back. She didn't wear a lot of makeup, but the organic, native jewelry she wore to compliment her simple black dress said a lot about her character. She wasn't afraid to be different. This woman was wholesome, positive and poised.

It soon became evident by conversations of the evening that she was also accomplished and smart. To Richard, that was sexy. Most of the women in the room were eye candy, with not much else to offer. They were beautiful, but had no interest or ability to carry on a meaningful, deep conversation. Their boundaries were small, stretching as far as a man's wallet would take them. Men like Richard usually preferred that. It made them feel superior. Richard saw Sydney as a challenge and quickly moved in to claim this trophy. He knew how to romance a woman.

Even though Sydney appeared confident, she was at a vulnerable point in her life. She had dated casually but hadn't had a serious relationship since her divorce. Richard and his gentlemanly manner easily swept her off her feet and in a few weeks of impressive romancing with concerts, museums, dining and dancing, they were a couple. He peaked her interest.

For a while Sydney thought Richard might be the one who could dissolve her insecurities and offer the type of relationship she longed for. At first he seemed perfect. He was attentive, romantic, and they had great conversations—the complete opposite from Mac's inability to show emotions or give her attention. Richard was an OK lover, but often was more interested in satisfying his own desires, his own fantasies. Sydney began to feel like his play toy, not the lover she longed to be. After a while she also discovered that Richard was possessive and controlling. She had grown too independent for that in the years since her divorce. She wanted an equal, not a bodyguard. She needed someone to excite her passion again, like in the early years of her marriage.

As Richard's facade of romantic nuances began to fade, Sydney realized she didn't know this man as well as she thought. She wasn't sure if she even really liked him. His personality was conflicting. There were signs of infidelity, fits of jealously, drinking too much, and domineering arguments when she went away on assignment for more than a few days at a time. This wasn't at all the relationship Sydney was looking for.

She'd tried several times to break it off, but Richard always had a way of gathering her back in. He was charming. Not many people said "no" to Richard and she wondered if she always came back because there was a little fear around their relationship. He had never been abusive, but she had seen his temper flare too many times and it concerned her. The relationship had become exhausting.

Sydney realized she had lost her spirit to the will of this man, and with this awareness she finally began to regain her strength. She had gotten up enough courage to face him and take back control of her life. It was time to reclaim her power, her independence. . .again. She confronted him when he came home late from work one day. He poured himself a drink and sat down.

"What's for dinner tonight?" he asked as he shuffled through the mail.

Sydney, standing before him, didn't answer.

"Is something bothering you?" he casually asked without looking up.

"I can't do this anymore, Richard. Our relationship just isn't working," she said flatly, trying to be firm. She looked him directly in the eyes.

Richard's first thought was that she had found out about a meaningless affair he was having with a co-worker, but he decided to play it cool. He gulped down whiskey from his glass and turned on the charm.

"Come on, Babe. You know you don't mean it. We've talked about this." He made a sweep of his arm to encompass his lavish apartment. "Why would you want to leave all this and go back to your small apartment?"

"This is what *you* want, Richard. Not me. We both know our relationship isn't working. There's no use to discuss it anymore, we've been over this before. There's nothing here for me and you have plenty of other interests. . ." she let her words hang so he understood she knew about his affair. "I wish you well, but I'm leaving you. Please don't try to contact me." She walked toward the door and reached for her bag.

Richard hadn't seen her suitcase when he came in. He grabbed her wrist and glared at her. Women didn't leave him. He was a good catch—wealthy, handsome, intelligent. He wasn't used to someone else calling the shots. He expected to be the dominant person in a relationship, at least until *he* was tired of it. What would people say, his friends, his colleagues? This blow to his ego was not sitting well.

"Sydney. Stop," he yelled.

"Let me go, Richard. I mean it. We're finished." Sydney read the anger on his face and all she wanted was to get as far away as possible while she still stood strong—before Richard's anger turned into rage. Friends had warned her of his moods, but she had chosen not to listen. Now, she understood their concern.

She pulled lose from his grip, quickly walked out the door and didn't look back. She heard him cussing as he slammed the door behind her. Throwing her overnight bag into the back seat, she sped away with a sigh of relief. She'd given him plenty of warning. This time he'd have to accept that she meant it. They were finished. It was over. Finally over.

She knew that Richard would be too proud to go after her and besides, he'd never find her where she was heading. It was her sanctuary.

~ three ~

SETTING BOUNDARIES

The Amazon may be the last place anyone would think of when wanting to retreat from the world, but it was just the place Sydney needed. She wanted the simplicity that only raw nature can produce. . . a place where there is no judgement, no pressure or ex-boyfriends. She needed the jungle.

Sydney arranged for a leave of absence from work without telling them where she was going. A vacation far from here, is all she alluded to. She had a friend who kept an eye on her apartment and watered plants whenever she was gone. Packing was easy. She had a system and a list. As much as she traveled, she kept many of her necessities in her suitcase so she only needed to add fresh clothing. She had learned how to travel light. However, there was one more thing she needed to do before she left.

Taking a long look at herself in the bathroom mirror, Sydney sighed. She grabbed the scissors from the drawer, reached back and cut off her long blonde braid. Symbolic, she thought. She needed a change. Her thick hair hung to just above her shoulders, with just enough length for a short ponytail. It would do. The hot jungle was no place for fashion.

Sydney wasn't a stranger to the rainforest. Her first trip to this remote part of the world was an assignment to photograph the research of scientists from the States. They were recording sound waves and energy patterns that vibrated from jungle plants that had little contact with humans. The research was highly technical and beyond Sydney's own scientific capacity, but she did her job, photographing the researchers and their project. In the process of her assignment, Sydney found the jungle exhilarating. She was hooked on the raw, unspoiled nature of the Amazon rainforest. After talking to friends about her amazing Amazon adventure, several people expressed interest in experiencing the jungle for themselves, which ultimately resulted in her leading dozens of group trips to Peru over the years. It wasn't for profit. It was because she loved the jungle, the villagers, and she was friends with the owners and staff at the jungle lodge.

Sydney brought people to the Amazon because she wanted them to experience it the way she had, before it was gone, disappeared in a cloud of civilization. Populations were dwindling and so were the villages. Some of the smaller settlements along the Amazon's tributary rivers had already shrunk to only a handful of palm-roofed huts. As village teenagers had opportunities to go down river 90-some miles to Iquitos for schooling, they didn't want to return to the native ways of their parents. City life had more appeal, more opportunities, excitement. It swallowed them up. Times were changing. Changing fast.

But this time Sydney was returning to the Amazon solo. She wanted to be alone with her misery. Her world was falling apart. . . again. Why did she always chose men who were unfaithful to her? Mac and now Richard. What kind of a reflection was that on her? What was wrong with her? For now, all she knew was that she wanted to escape. She needed solitude.

It was an exhausting journey, flying from New York to Lima, to Iquitos. This busy, noisy city of 750,000 people is where Sydney would begin her boat journey on the Amazon River toward her destination, deep in the jungle. Iquitos, located in northeast Peru, in the far western Amazon forest, is surrounded by impenetrable jungle and is the world's largest city not connected to any other city by road. The only way to get to Iquitos is by air or by river. Sydney liked that sense of seclusion.

Once the hustle and bustle of noisy airports ended and Sydney stepped aboard "Stephanie," the canopied wooden speedboat that would transport her to the Amazonia Tahuayo River Lodge, she relaxed. Her world calmed as the Amazon River greeted her and cloaked her within its serene beauty. She would be traveling four hours up the Amazon River and then off on a smaller tributary, the Tahuayo, a region referred to as "the green paradise."

Sydney was a true believer in visualization and manifesting what she wanted and needed in her life. Most of the time it was effortless. She had landed a successful job that enabled her to travel and explore other cultures. She had creative outlets through her photography and her writing, and she had many good friends. She seemed to be tuned in to what the Universe had planned for her and was pretty good at following her intuition. But her romantic life had never been that easy. She hadn't been able to find that balance. She admittedly learned something from each relationship and consoled herself that they were lessons for her own growth. Each of those lessons, however, seemed to leave an emotional scar, and after her recent failed relationship with Richard, Sydney was ready to give up on love all together. She was grateful to have men friends and colleagues in her life, so had masculine energy around when she needed it. Maybe the love she longed for after all, was within herself. Maybe she should be satisfied being alone without a mate. It seemed like a good idea.

Now, on the boat, before heading deep into her jungle retreat, Sydney closed her eyes and recalled that before she left New York, she took time to sit in meditation, seeking clarity in her life. She went deep inside herself and wondered if before she could find that true love she yearned for, she had to first find a way to love herself more. She had to become her own true love.

On the outside she looked confident and secure, but on the inside she was searching to find herself, to overcome the insecurities of her past and love herself for the person she had worked hard to become. Maybe that wasn't enough. Maybe the distraction of men collided with her acceptance of herself and kept her from battling and conquering her own demons. She decided that in order for her to concentrate on mending her own inner conflicts, she should take away the distractions that seemed to cause more distress and create more wounds. One failed relationship was bad enough, but two was more than she could handle. She decided the best solution was to give up men - for at least one year.

At least she'd try. . .

~ four ~
FINDING PARADISE

Sydney broke her thoughtful trance and looked around at the other passengers on the boat—a small group of college kids, boys eager for exploration; six lively senior citizens; and two men, who she had been told were doctors. Often physicians, nurses and dentists came to volunteer in the clinic in Esperanza Village to help in whatever way they could. Good health care was always needed in the jungle. Local shaman and herbalists continued to work their healing wonders in every day life, as had been done for generations in these native villages, but sometimes, especially in the case of broken bones and minor surgeries, traditional medicine was a necessary solution. Iquitos was several days by canoe, so the cement block Esperanza Clinic served all the local villages for miles around. . .river miles and jungle miles.

Four hours to the jungle camp by boat may sound like a long time to a new guest, but Sydney always enjoyed the boat ride, taking plenty of photographs along the way. There was a lot to see as they maneuvered through the port in Iquitos and veered into the dirty waters of the Amazon. Boats of all sizes, shapes and ages traveled these waters, carrying wares to and from the city. Fishing boats, dugout canoes, crude rafts piled high with bananas and other fruit to sell in the open markets, old rusty freighters that now housed river dwellers, all found places in the harbor. There were no fancy sailboats or speedy motorboats. This was a working port. There were also simple tourist cruise boats that traveled up and down the river, stopping for brief times at some of the villages. This is how many of the natives made money, by selling handmade baskets, fragile pottery and jungle jewelry to tourists.

The wooden Amazonia Lodge boat with "Stephanie" painted on the side was named after the daughter of Paul and Dolly, owners of the jungle lodge. It was comfortable, had inside seating for shade, or guests could take turns sitting out in the sun in the bow, but most importantly, the boat had a bathroom. Sydney smiled at the huge pile of luggage stacked in the rear of the boat. Her backpack was nestled among the suitcases. She was glad she traveled light.

They passed thatched roof huts along the way, with women out washing their clothes in the river. Often times children would stand along the riverbanks and wave as the boats passed by. They swam naked in the dirty brown water of the Amazon, bathed in it and dipped their tin cans into it to carry water to their houses where they boiled it to cook their meals and wash dishes. This was the same water where snakes, electric eel, piranha and a multitude of other reptiles and mammals lived, including caiman, a form of crocodile.

Sydney loved the sights and smells of the river and wanted to enjoy the ride, but she was exhausted and just couldn't keep her eyes open. She tipped her wide brimmed hat down over her face and tried to catch some sleep. She wasn't interested in conversation. There would be plenty of time for that. Guests had a way of mingling at meals and spilling out their life stories. She knew. She'd brought almost 100 tourists here in the past few years. It was good therapy.

Her solitude didn't last long.

"Excuse me, Miss," one of the doctors politely said. "I'm sorry to interrupt your rest, but I was asked to give you one of these stylish, bright orange life jackets." He chuckled.

Sydney groaned under her breath, but not wanting to be rude, she slowly lifted the brim of her hat for a brief response. Her mood quickly changed as deep green eyes met hers. She was taken aback by the gentleness behind them-—and the tan, handsome face next to her. It made her heart flutter.

Once he had her attention, the man wasted no time in drawing her into conversation.

"I also noticed you talking with the river guides earlier, like you knew them. Have you been to the jungle lodge before?"

"Yes, a few times," Sydney slowly responded. "I've been there a few times." She sat up in her seat, trying to keep her composure as the man slid into the empty space next to her. His arm lightly brushed against hers and it sent involuntary shivers down her spine.

"Whoa. Settle down, Sydney," she told herself, surprised that such a simple touch could trigger her senses so quickly. "Let's be sensible here, not irrational." She silently chanted, "One year, one year, one year" over and over in her mind.

"I really didn't mean to interrupt your rest," the man apologized again, noticing her uneasiness. "But there's so much to see out there on the river, I was surprised you weren't soaking it all in. Then I realized you must have been here before. Are you in the medical field or maybe a teacher coming here to help in the village school?" He had been watching her since she got on the boat and knew she must have an interesting story behind that pretty face.

"No," Sydney answered, reclaiming her calm. "I wish it were that valiant. I bring groups of people down here on occasion. It's such an adventure and an eye-opener into a simpler way of life. I like sharing it with others. But, we usually do bring things for the children and villagers, including medical and school supplies."

"Are some of these other travelers with you?" the man inquired, gesturing toward others in the boat.

"Oh no. This time I'm traveling alone," Sydney revealed.

"I'm Drew," the man smiled and held out his hand. "Drew Harris."

She stared at him, reminding herself once again that she had recently vowed to give up men for one year. . .one long year.

"Nice to meet you, Drew. I'm Sydney Knight," she reached out to accept his handshake—taking note of his sturdy, yet soft hand. She responded with a firm grip, letting him know she was a strong, independent woman. Or maybe because, at that moment, she needed to confirm that for herself.

"What brings you here?" she asked. "Have you been to the jungle before?"

"I haven't been here, but yes, I have been to the jungle before. I'm a doctor and have traveled with teams of physicians to Borneo, Belize and Bolivia, among other places. My friend Reagan is also a doctor," he motioned toward his friend who was chatting with some of the college students. "We work together. We thought it would be good to get away from the grind of the hospital for awhile and if we can be of assistance while here, well, that's even better," Drew said, not being completely honest in his answer.

Sydney wondered if they were gay, two men traveling together. That would make it so much easier for her. She couldn't help her instant attraction to him. He was so damn handsome.

Drew was almost six foot tall, clean shaven and with his muscular physique, there was no denying that he worked out. His light brown hair was thick and unruly, shaggy with a hint of curl around his ears. Not at all a typical doctor haircut. Windblown locks of hair fell over his forehead and Sydney had all she could do, not to reach up and push it out of the way to reveal the full intensity of those green eyes. She looked away.

"Well, I'm sure the villagers will appreciate your help, even if you only volunteer for a day or two at the clinic. Even with their dedicated staff, there's never enough health care to go around. If it weren't for Paul and Dolly, owners of the Tahuayo River Lodge, and all they do to help, the area natives would have a much harder life." She added, "I hope you enjoy your visit."

"I know I will. I read on their website about how the lodge got its start, with Paul coming to the Amazon from the States as a biologist years ago, starting a tourist business and eventually marrying Dolly, who is native Peruvian. It's quite a success story when you think of how they help support and educate people in so many ways."

"I see you've done your research," Sydney replied. It was easy for her to talk about the jungle lodge. She respected the owners and didn't mind bragging about them. "Yes, they not only educate local natives on how to be excellent guides, but they also help the villages in their area. They run a very respected jungle destination and have been rated number one in Amazon lodges for years. They also have a research facility that attracts scientists from around the world. They're the real thing"

"I can hardly wait to get there and learn more," the doctor said.

Sydney was extremely tired and chalked up her sudden sensory attraction to his man to vulnerability in her state of exhaustion. "I don't mean to be rude," she said. "But I really could use some sleep before we get there. It's been a very long day." Avoidance seemed to be the best medicine.

"Of course. I'm sorry. I didn't mean to intrude. We'll have plenty of time to visit once we arrive," he said, unable to keep his eyes off her—but he didn't move back to his own seat. He wanted to stay close to her. He definitely needed to get to know this intriguing woman.

Sydney tipped the brim of her hat back down over her face. It hid the smile that crossed her lips as her tongue licked the inner edges of her mouth, but the hat couldn't mask her sigh of hot breath that followed. She would have to be very careful on this trip. This she knew.

~~~~~

The usual four hour trip to the Tahuayo Lodge stretched into over five hours due to low water levels and sandbars in some areas of the Amazon River. The boatmen knew the river like the back of their hands. They grew up on the Amazon and her tributaries. As darkness closed in, Arturo, the driver navigated with a single headlamp with one of the river guides sitting at the bow, giving hand directions to indicate logs and low spots on the river, signaling to veer left or right. They traveled 50 miles up the mighty Amazon River and had 40 miles left once they curved left onto the Tahuayo River.

When Sydney awoke, she could see the guests were a becoming nervous, as it got darker and later.

Her "travel guide" mind set in to help the staff ease any fears the guests might have. She trusted the boatman and staff completely and knew they would get them to the lodge safely. She'd been through this several times before. Sydney turned around and made conversation to help pass the time, sharing stories of her past adventures and of how incredible the lodge would be when they finally arrived. Her calm attitude replaced the guest's nervousness with laughter. The knowledgeable staff on the boat answered a lot of questions about the lodge and activities and everyone seemed to become at ease.

Sydney couldn't help but feel Drew's eyes on her while she spoke and for a weak moment she wished she had someone special to share her adventure. But no, she was retreating into the jungle to get away from men, not to complicate her life with another affair.

~ five ~

DEMONS OF THE NIGHT

Sydney was right about the first spectacular sight of the lodge as they approached it in the dark of the night. As the boat finally rounded the last bend in the river, they could see lanterns lining the walkways of the lodge, greeting visitors with a romantic glow of life.

Arriving at the lodge was always a pleasure. The staff was friendly and came out to greet their guests with cold fruit drinks and genuine hospitality. Sydney had known many of the staff for years and looked forward to catching up with news of their lives and families. Many of the staff were from neighboring villages. All were native Peruvian. After a welcome dinner in the screened-in dining hall, guests followed the wooden walkways that led to their rooms. Each of the lodge's fifteen cabins were raised above the jungle floor on stilts and connected to other buildings of the lodge by a raised boardwalk that was covered with thatched roofing. It was practical and charming. Sydney knew that the doctor wanted to talk with her, but she wasn't up for it. She kept busy visiting with her old friends from the lodge and was glad to quietly slip away to her room shortly after dinner.

Refreshed from a cool shower, Sydney draped the mosquito netting over her bed and settled in for a good night's sleep. The staff always arranged for her to have the same room each time she visited, so she felt at home. The heat of the day had subdued after a rain shower and the evening temps lowered at least ten degrees. But sleep did not last long. It wasn't the chorus of frogs and cicadas that kept her from the deep sleep she so needed. It was a dream that painted a vivid picture and wouldn't let her mind rest. The scene was familiar, a nightmare from her past, but this time it was different, violent, so out of character for Sydney and even more disturbing than the reality of the marriage she couldn't forget.

— Sydney left work early and as she drove in the yard she saw Janet's car parked next to Mac's in the driveway. She walked into the house and seeing Janet's shoes in the entry, she picked them up and threw them into the garbage can. She walked directly into the bedroom and stood in the doorway for a few moments. She watched Mac, his muscular frame raised above Janet, as he groaned and thrust his maleness into her. Her arms were around him, urging him to go faster, deeper. . .and at that moment Sydney calmly walked into the room, opened the closet door and reached up on the shelf where Mac kept his loaded 22 pistol. She took pleasure in disrupting their lovemaking as Mac rolled to the side and Janet struggled to grab a sheet to cover her naked body.

"What the f. . ." Mac started to say.

"Exactly," Sydney finished his sentence as she aimed the pistol at them. Janet screamed. Then Sydney slowly turned and, framing Mac and Janet in the reflection of the mirror above the dresser, she deliberately fired two shots. Glass flew everywhere as the mirror shattered into pieces, leaving no trace of the astonished couple in its view. Mac was

dumbfounded. Janet covered her head with the sheet and screamed hysterically.

Sydney calmly turned and walked into the bathroom, closing and locking the door behind her. She saw Mac and Janet's clothing in a heap on the floor, which was still wet from their shower together. She scooped up Janet's clothes and opening the window, she pushed out the screen and threw the clothes onto the lawn. Then she grabbed Janet's purse and, before she threw it to join the clothes on the grass, she pulled out the makeup bag and dumped its contents into the toilet. She also removed Janet's driver's license from her wallet and threw that in with the makeup, and then flushed the toilet. Symbolic, she thought. Janet was a married woman. She deserved to lose her identity.

Next she took Mac's joint-account checkbook and wallet out of his pants. She removed his credit cards and his cash, almost $500, leaving him $1. She could hear them in the next room, scrambling to get dressed. Mac yelled at Janet to get out before Sydney did something else drastic. Janet yelled that her clothes were in the bathroom. Mac threw her a pair of Sydney's sweatpants and a T-shirt and shouted for at her to leave.

Sydney stood looking at herself in the mirror. The image that looked back at her was filled with questions.

"What's wrong with me? Am I ugly? Boring? Am I too fat? Why?"

Sydney raised the pistol and pulled the trigger. She could hear Janet scream.

"My God. Oh my God!" Mac shouted as he pounded on the door. "Sydney!"

Glass from the mirror shattered all around Sydney. She stood staring, trancelike into a fractured mosaic of her reflection on broken shards of glass on the floor. Mac broke down the door and reached for the pistol.

"For Christ sake, Sydney. . ." he yelled, but she pulled her hand away and looked directly into his eyes with defiance. She said nothing, quickly walking past him, out of the bedroom and out of the house—her house. Mac started to follow her, but Janet grabbed his arm. "It's not safe," she warned him. "She's gone mad. Let her cool down first. She still has the gun for God's sake!"

Sydney backed her car out of the driveway and before she drove away, she fired four more shots. Both back tires on Janet's car and on Mac's pick-up truck sizzled and went flat. She knew they had only one spare for each vehicle. Four flat tires would take time to fix. She drove to the end of the driveway and placing the empty pistol in a plastic shopping bag from her trunk, she hid it deep in the bushes. Then she calmly dialed Janet's husband, Jeff, on her cell phone and told him that she had just caught Janet and Mac together in bed. He should come right over.

But the dream—or was it a nightmare—didn't end there.

Sydney drove to the bank, transferred half of the money from their savings account into her private checking account and wrote a check for cash for half of the money in their joint checking account. She called her boss to arrange for time off work and drove away. She needed time to figure this out. After all, she really didn't like confrontation. ——

Sydney woke up in a cold sweat. She was visibly shaken.

"What the hell? Where did this come from?" she questioned. She had been divorced for years. Why was she having a dream like this now? Why does she have to revisit these demons of her past? She took a gulp of water from the bottle on her nightstand and sat shaking, contemplating this nightmare. It brought back such painful memories of the time she really did catch Mac and Janet together—and just walked away, avoiding the obvious. Avoiding the conflict.

She opened her mosquito netting and sat on the edge of her bed. How could she go back to sleep after this? She covered her face with her hands and rubbed her eyes, trying to erase the horrible visions. Tears began to form.

"Damn him," she said. "Damn them both. Why can't I let loose of my failure to be loved? Why does it have to keep haunting me? What's wrong with me?"

Sydney began to pace the floor like a woman possessed, talking to herself, trying to shake the intense scene that had just played out in her mind.

"Why?" she repeated.

Just then she caught the reflection of herself in the bathroom mirror. She walked over and stood before it, less than a foot away and looked directly into her own eyes. She stared into those eyes for the longest time as if she were hypnotized by her mirror image. Suddenly the lines on her face began to soften. She continued to gaze at herself as if the person looking back at her was someone else—someone who was beaming a light of pure love into her. Loving her for who she was and how she looked and for everything she stood for. Telling there was nothing wrong with her. She was loved. She was enough.

Then slowly, Sydney began to smile. The woman in her reflection smiled back. Sydney understood. The affirmation in the mirror told her that there was nothing wrong with her, that she should stop questioning herself—no more why, what's wrong with me? No more insecurities as she moved forward to seek that balance in her life she so desperately wanted. The love she was longing for was inside herself. Pure, unconditional love. It was there all the time. She just had to accept it. She *was* love.

Maybe, just maybe, this horrible dream was the closure she wasn't able to find before, the confrontation she had avoided. If she could never confront this demon of a relationship in real life, maybe she had just found that closure, uncharacteristically dramatic and violent, in her unconscious reality, through a dream. What else could it be? Was she now free of the trust issues that bound her and the inability to allow her to give herself wholly to another man? Could this love inside her unite her with her soulmate?

One thing Sydney knew for sure. If she was destined to be alone, it was all right. She had found her own true love. It was deep inside herself all the time. She was all she ever wanted. She was loved.

~ six ~
JUNGLE LIFE

Drew retreated to his room after dinner, but couldn't get the image of Sydney out of his head. He didn't come here looking for love and had never been smitten with a woman like this before. Was it because she ignored him? Was it because she seemed so worldly and mysterious? Or simply because she was so casual about life? He had seated himself across from her at dinner, yet didn't get a chance to visit. She was polite, nodding at him now and then to include him in her conversation and listening to his responses, but it was obvious she didn't have the same attraction he felt. He knew he would be better off trying to ignore her and continue on this adventure with his friend Reagan, volunteering in the clinic as they had planned, fishing, hiking, canopy zip lining and enjoying all the brochure had offered. He wouldn't give her another thought. . .

Why would she be interested in him anyhow? They had just met. He was a doctor who had spent all his time working. He had little experience with women. He was married while still in college and it was a happy time in his life. They were young and carefree and very much in love. When his wife suddenly died, Drew was devastated and felt helpless. That's when he decided to go to medical school and become a doctor. Saving lives became his focus and he had little room for anything else. He was driven. It helped to bury the pain of losing his young wife. Granted, it had been years since her death, but he had only dated a few times since and that was because friends had dragged him on a double date with someone he just "had to meet." It never turned out well. He was a lost cause. Why should he expect this to be anything different— other than the fact that he felt that twinge— something he never thought he'd experience again in his life. Maybe it was time for him to explore. Maybe he was ready, even if it was just a short affair. It might be just what the doctor ordered.

Drew's emptiness since his wife's death wasn't his only setback. He had other demons to deal with. Recent ones. He was haunted by an incident at work that caused him to be suspended for a time. He wanted to walk away from the hospital after that, but times were tough. He lived simply, but he still had old student loans from medical school to pay off. He had to swallow his pride and conform to the rules of big hospital hierarchy. That's part of the reason he came here. He needed to get away and he was grateful his colleague Reagan stood with him when he needed a friend.

Drew let down the mosquito netting around his bed as he settled in. He punched the pillow to fluff it up and lay back, focusing on the screened roof of the hut. At first the volume of noise from the jungle annoyed him—frogs, bugs, animals calling in the night. Then he slowly let his muscles relax and enjoyed the music of nature. Through the screen window he could see the open river with a cloud of stars above the treetops, blazing across the sky. It had been a long time since he had seen such a light show in the dark of night and he was mesmerized by the brilliance of the jungle moon as it drew a yellow road across the length of the Tahuayo River.

Somewhere in the distance he heard music floating through the air from a Peruvian flute. Gentle, soothing, earthy music that soon drifted his thoughts away and sent him into a sound, peaceful sleep.

~~~~~

The morning brought a much brighter outlook for everyone. That was another thing Sydney appreciated about the jungle. You went to bed when it was dark and awoke when the sun came up. No alarm clocks to keep you on track—only the first light of dawn and the banging of the drum to announce that breakfast was served.

Sydney was the last to arrive in the dining hall. She generously filled her plate from the buffet table, heaping it with scrambled eggs, fried plantain, manioc—which the locals call yuca (yoo-ca), and a mix of fresh papaya, mango, bananas and other fruits, along with a glass of passion fruit juice. She knew the food here was alway delicious and fresh. Kudos to the chef and kitchen staff, she thought, knowing she'd eat healthy with no preservatives or chemicals tainting the food. Sydney wasn't a vegetarian or a food prude, but she did read labels.

She tried to stick to fresh foods as much as she could. She loved to eat and was round about the edges because of it, but she was healthy and active and wasn't concerned about her weight, especially when she was on vacation. Right now she was starving, and in her present state of mind if someone handed her a bag of Cheetos or a box of Hostess cupcakes, she'd probably gobble them all down before thinking.

She scanned the happy guests at the tables as she looked for a place to sit and hoped she wouldn't encounter Doctor Drew this morning. She couldn't help the attraction she so quickly had felt for him and thought the best thing to do would be to avoid him as much as possible, even though he had been on her mind since sunup. Whether her pistol toting nightmare had been a clearing house for what was to come, she didn't know, but she had promised herself no relationships for a year. . . and it had been less than a week. It was ridiculous. She had just met this man.

Sydney glanced at the chalk board on the wall with events scheduled for the day. It was a great way to plan an itinerary. Each evening after dinner the next day's events were listed on the board. Slash marks were made as guests raised their hands to sign up. This let the staff know how many guides they would need for each event and allowed them time to work out their schedules. If guests wanted to do something else, it was added to the board. The staff was very accommodating. Sydney recalled when two of her travelers one year were potters and inquired if there was a local potter in a nearby village. The next day an elderly woman who made pots from riverbank clay was located and plans were made for the two women to spend a day with her. In the Amazon, anything seems possible.

This morning's events listed on the board were:

6 a.m. - bird watching by canoe

7 a.m. - canopy zip lining

9 a.m. - jungle hiking to terra firme
       with picnic lunch

11 a.m. - medicinal jungle walk with local herbalist

1 p.m. - lunch

2 p.m. - fishing

Sydney surmised that Drew had signed up for one of those events, or possibly had already headed to the clinic to begin his work. She refused to admit disappointment at not seeing him at breakfast.

After a relaxing morning of reading in the hammock room, photographing around the lodge and visiting with staff, Sydney realized that she was not cut out for just laying around and doing nothing as she had originally planned. She had experienced all of the activities many times, but each time the adventure was different. She didn't want to waste her jungle time. The place was simply too exciting. After lunch she joined a small group heading out to fish for piranha in a nearby lake.

Sydney always loved watching people's reactions as they caught piranha. The process was simple. A thin branch was stripped and used as a pole, tied with nylon fishing line and a hook with bait—usually a chunk of fresh meat. The fisherman or fisherwoman swished the end of the pole in the water, making a splash, and then waited for a fish to come see what was happening. It sounded simple, but it worked! Chef would have plenty of fish to cook for dinner tonight. And nothing was wasted in the jungle. Piranha jawbones, with those very sharp teeth, were handy. They were used to sharpen the tips of darts, which were used in blow guns for hunting small game. The razor-sharp piranha teeth were used for cutting hair and separating plant fibers from palm leaves to make string. Sometimes the jawbone and teeth appeared in handmade jungle jewelry.

The afternoon was filled with laughter, fish to fry, and making new friends. Cousins, Bev and JoAnn, along with their friend, Rita, were part of the senior citizen group from Minnesota. They were married women, traveling together without husbands. Sydney found them delightful company. Jean and Steve were a couple, and the sixth person in their group was a single man, Adam, who was very dashing and in his own mind was very much a lady's man. Each of the women were very independent, secure and full of life. None were interested in starting an affair, still, they each enjoyed the flirtatious atmosphere within their group with Adam. They had all been friends for years. Sydney envied their interaction. It was easy, fun and healthy. Non-threatening. She could learn a lot from these women.

Conversation was lively at dinner that evening with everyone sharing their day's excitement and planning what adventures they would sign up for next. Sydney shared the digital photographs she had documented of the day's fishing adventure and promised to email copies once she had a chance. People bonded so easily here with no agenda. Friendships were quickly made with no assessments of a person's past, their shortcomings or achievements. Everyone was equal. Sydney joined in the conversation, but couldn't help keep an eye out for Drew. Where was he? Had she misjudged his attraction to her? That's it. She was spending all this time trying to avoid her attraction to him, that she hadn't thought it might not be mutual. He was a doctor. He just had a friendly bedside manner. She was acting like an infatuated school girl.

"Stop it Sydney. What's gotten into you?" she scolded herself, vowing to ignore him when she ran into him. He, and his gorgeous green eyes, must have made arrangements to spend the entire time at the clinic in Esperanza Village, several miles down river from the lodge. That would solve her problem. Anyhow, she came here to get away from men, to relax.

seven

THE HÆMMOCK ROOM

Drew was exhausted from his day, but at the same time he was overjoyed. He did what he does best. Work. He and his colleague, Reagan, had risen early and were transported by boat to the clinic to spend the day delivering supplies they had collected from the States, evaluating needs and making preliminary assessments with the clinic's medical staff. It was meant to be a half day's evaluation and they would begin to see patients the next day. They would spend a week at the clinic, working for a few hours each day and try to find some adventure time in between shifts. That didn't look promising.

Already they had encountered several emergency situations—delivering a breach baby, dealing with a child who had a severe foot infection, stitching up a machete wound and diagnosing a woman who thought she was going blind, but most likely needed cataract surgery. The two doctors assisted the competent clinic staff seeing dozens of patients, young and old, throughout the day.

Drew and Reagan were amazed at how much the clinic personnel did with less than modern resources. The clinic's small staff worked endlessly and looked forward to occasional outside help for diagnosis, feedback and assistance in patient treatment. No insurance paperwork here. No red tape or fear of being sued. No writing prescriptions. Just doing what a medical staff is trained to do— provide treatment and care for the sick, payment or not, with instant gratification on both sides. Everyone was here to help.

The two men, along with Augusto, their jungle guide and interpreter, arrived back at the lodge well after dark. Their boatman, Arturo, cut the engine on the boat as soon as they were in range of the camp, so as not to awaken the sleeping guests. The boat glided into its docking area with a little muscle behind a pair of handmade heart-shaped jungle paddles. Exhausted nods were acknowledged as the men headed off to their quarters and the guides tended to the boat.

Drew paused as he passed by Sydney's door. He wondered if she was still awake, if she heard his lingering footsteps? He hesitated a few moments and then continued down the creaking boardwalk to his room. He helped save the life of a mother and her baby today. The gratification of that should be enough to satisfy him. In the past it would have been all he needed to feel fulfilled. To feel needed. Yet now, he longed for something more. Something certainly not as important as saving lives, but something important to make his own life, beyond his work, worth living. He couldn't get the image of Sydney Knight out of his mind.

~~~~~

It was 2 a.m. and Drew was still awake. He had only a few hours before breakfast and his boat ride back to the clinic. He knew he should try to sleep, but was too restless. He pulled on a pair of shorts and didn't bother to button his shirt. He headed to the hammock room, hoping he could curl up in the cocoon of a hammock and rock himself to sleep. He'd always thought hammocks were nurturing. As he entered the room and guided the wooden screen door quietly shut he saw a hammock slowly rocking to and fro. Not wanting to disturb the other person, he turned to leave.

"Drew?" a voice whispered. "Is that you?"

Drew stepped closer and was surprised to find Sydney cozily nestled in the center of a colorfully striped hammock.

"Whatever are you doing here?" he asked.

"Probably the same as you," she replied. "I couldn't sleep. I love being wrapped in the arms of a hammock. It's comforting."

"I know what you mean," he said. "I hope I didn't alarm or disturb you."

"Oh, no. Pull up a hammock. Looks like we're the only insomniacs here."

Drew settled into the woven mesh next to Sydney. It was useless to try to sleep with her so near. He had positioned himself at the opposite end of his hammock so he could see her. So he could watch her sleep. He waited as long as he could, but he just had to talk with her.

"Sydney. Are you asleep?" he whispered.

"Yes," she replied and they began to laugh.

"Shhh," she said. "We'll wake the other guests."

"I thought we were the only ones in here," he playfully quipped.

"You know what I mean."

Propping themselves up in their hammocks so they were facing each other, they stared blankly for a few awkward moments. Finally Drew broke the silence.

"I was hoping to be able to spend some time with you. I just didn't expect we'd be sleeping together." He quickly retracted, "I'm sorry. I can't believe I even said that. It's so out of character for me. Please, it wasn't a come-on. It just slipped out."

Sydney smiled. She kind of liked seeing him feel uncomfortable—out of the suave doctor character she imagined.

"It was a pretty corny line," she replied. "Is that your usual bedside manner?"

"No, believe me. I'm really pretty boring. I haven't had much time for anything like that. My life is my work. My work is my life."

"That surprises me. I thought maybe you were one of those dashing doctor types who collects swooning women and keeps them at your fingertips."

"Ouch. That bites," Drew replied. "You've got me all wrong. How about you? Are you one of those women who collects men as she journeys around the world, loves them and leaves them in a trail of travel dust?"

"Ha!" Sydney scoffed. "You aren't even warm."

"Then, who are you Sydney Knight? And why am I so attracted to you—other than the fact that you're so beautiful?" Again, Drew was surprised at his own boldness.

"My, you are quite aggressive, Dr Harris."

"I'm sorry. I don't know what's come over me. I'm just curious why you're here and why you're traveling alone. Is there no Mr. Knight?"

"There was a Mr. Knight quite some time ago. It took me years to realize he wasn't my knight in shining armor. It's complicated. We were childhood sweethearts. The old familiar story of getting married too young and all that. He's remarried. We're friends. That's the most I would hope for. . . I. . .I have a lot of scars from that marriage I haven't fully recovered from. It makes relationships difficult for me. Trust. Vulnerability. Like I said, it's complicated. Anyhow. I'm very independent. I don't need a man in my life to complete me."

"Oh, spoken like a true feminist," Drew replied.

"Not really. Of course I support women's rights, but I have all I can do to take care of myself these days. I've had a great career, but am winding down a bit, trying to find my center, to balance my life. If that makes any sense."

"It sounds like there's a lot more to you than I expected. I'd like to hear more," Drew responded, his eyes fixed on hers.

"How about you," Sydney changed the subject, uncomfortable talking about her personal life. She'd already blurted out more than she expected.

"What's your story? Married? Kids?" Now she was fishing.

Drew sat silent for a long time, pondering how much he wanted to share. He never talked much about his private life, but for some reason, he was compelled to bring it to the surface.

Finally he spoke, slowly and deliberately. "I loved my wife more than anything else in the world. We grew up together and married while still in college. We had some very happy years together." He paused. Remembering was painful.

"What happened?" Sydney could feel his emotion. He was sensitive and that was appealing to her.

"Why did you break up?"

"She died," he answered abruptly. After a moment of silence, he continued. "It was sudden. It started as a chest cold. It turned into pneumonia and got progressively worse with infections after she was in the hospital. I lost her inside of a few weeks. I couldn't believe it." Drew shifted in his hammock. "That's when I decided to become a doctor. I've dedicated myself to helping others and haven't had much of a life other than work since."

Sydney didn't quite know what to say. "I'm sorry, Drew. It must have been hard for you."

"Her parents blamed me until the day they died. They said I should have brought her to the doctor sooner. Maybe they were right. How could we have known? She said it was a lingering cold. We were just dumb kids. Maybe it was my fault," his words trailed away. He'd never quite forgiven himself and hadn't voiced his fear of being at fault. He finally cleared his voice.

"I'll never really know for sure. It's in the past now. I've just had trouble moving forward."

"You have scars too," Sydney said with empathy. Realizing they had a lot in common—a lot to work through. She reached over to his hammock and placed her hand on his.

"Do you believe in destiny? That experience caused you to changed your studies and you became a physician. Look how many people you've helped since then. You're a dedicated doctor. That counts for a lot. For everything, really."

Drew gave a sigh. "Thanks. I don't usually share my past like this, so if you don't mind, keep it to yourself, please."

"The same here. I don't talk about my past much either, although it's probably good therapy," Sydney said, pulling her hand away before the heat of her fingertips found its way through her body.

Drew grasped her hand. "You have a pretty good bedside manner yourself," he said, coming out of his blue mood.

"You're pretty flirty after what you just told me. Get my sympathy and then make your move. What's that about?" She asked as she reluctantly freed her hand.

"I don't know what's gotten into me. I just feel playful around you. Believe me, it's new for me.

Ask Reagan. He'll vouch for my virgin personality and boring lifestyle."

"I'll do just that," Sydney responded, laughing at him.

The two travelers casually talked into the night, swinging gently in their hammocks, listening to the lapping of the water on the shore of the river and the boat bumping against the dock, sounding like a deep drum to the chorus of frogs and katydids singing in the darkness. The song of a frog-mouth bird called a Paraque was dominate in the distance, making its hauntingly beautiful call, "Tah-why-ooo, Tah-why-ooo," from which the river's name, Tahuayo, is derived.

While Sydney and Drew cloaked their mutual attraction for each other in conversation, sharing travel stories, life in New York and other interests, they found they had many things in common—favorite restaurants, music, art. Dialogue was fluid and they didn't run out of things to talk and laugh about. They kept the conversation light, but there was electricity in the air that neither could deny.

Sydney watched Drew closely as he spoke, studying his body language, his mannerisms. She could feel the heat rise in her body as she thought about how it would be to lie next to him, to feel his body tight against her, his lips on hers, his breath in her mouth. She found herself drifting into an exotic fantasy with Drew's conversation as soft background music to their lovemaking.

"I. . . I'm sorry, what did you say?" she said, shaking her head to bring herself back to reality.

"It's OK," he replied, watching her just as intensely. "I think we're both tired. I don't want to bore you."

"Oh, you're not boring me at all. I just drifted off into another thought for a moment. I'm sorry. I really am interested in what you have to say. I guess the night is catching up with me."

Dawn was near and neither had slept a wink.

"This was the best night I've had in years," Drew said. "I've really enjoyed not sleeping with you tonight."

Sydney smiled. "Before you get any ideas," she warned him, and reminded herself, "I should tell you that I've recently come out of a bad relationship and I've sworn off men for an entire year."

Drew laughed.

"No, I'm serious," she retorted, trying to set boundaries to help keep the promise she made to herself, before she completely gave in to Drew's charms and her fantasies. "So let's get this clear. I like you a lot. I like talking with you and tonight was really special, but I'm not in the market for a relationship with anyone just now. I came here to find myself, to find that balance I was talking about."

Drew replied with a smirk, "Just out of curiosity, when is your year up?"

". . .I'll let you know," Sydney answered coyly, keeping her options open.

"Fine. Friends then. I like spending time with you too. I'm glad we had this conversation. It takes the edge off of trying to impress you, to figure you out—wondering how you feel and all that."

"I think I'd better go back to my room. It doesn't look like either of us are going to get any sleep out here tonight," Sydney said. "Or should I say this morning?" She gestured toward the horizon.

They laughed as they sat up and ungracefully attempted to crawl out of their respective hammocks, but instead tumbled onto the wooden floorboards. Drew landed on the floor first, with Sydney clumsily piling on top of him. Suddenly their moods changed. Time slowed down. Drew felt

Sydney's braless breasts through her clothing crushing onto his chest. His shirt was open and her body rubbed against his bare skin. The neckline of her tank top gave way to reveal her full, succulent bosom. The hot curves of her body filled into the flesh of his torso and he could feel himself involuntarily responding to her closeness through the thin fabric of his shorts. She felt it too. Their thoughts were in sync. All they wanted to do was grind into the bones of each other's body, hold each other tight and drown themselves in saturated kisses and feverish passion.

Drew was so close to Sydney's lips that she could feel his heavy breath on her mouth. Their eyes awkwardly met. Sydney slowly moved her body, her thoughts running wild, not wanting to pull herself away from him, but instead wanting to wriggle and rub herself all over his muscular body, feeling the heat of his bare skin and the intensity of his maleness. She shuddered with excitement. She knew what she had to do. She just had to. Slowly rolling to one side, her hair gently brushed the side of Drew's face. He was going wild with desire, but before he could pull her to him, before he could take her into his arms and appease his raging appetite, Sydney found her footings and unsteadily moved away.

"I. . .I'm sorry," she stuttered. Slowly moving toward the door.

Quickly rising to his feet, Drew reached for her hand, trying to recover from his eagerness.

"No. Don't be sorry. It was my clumsiness. I didn't mean to react like that. . . I mean. . .that was pretty intense." He was searching for words. "I hope I didn't offend you," he offered, knowing full well that she was just as hungry for him. That was undeniable.

"Oh, no," she responded, heaving a deep sigh to control her breath. "But I think you'll agree that we better leave before things get out of hand and we both get burned by our impulses. I can't deny the attraction, Drew, but I just told you, I'm in recovery. You wouldn't want to be my rebound man."

"Oh, I don't think that would be such a bad thing," he smiled. "I could handle that." He hoped he didn't sound too eager.

"But I couldn't," she replied.

"I understand, Sydney. I respect you and don't want this to get in the way of our new friendship. Strangely, I feel like I've known you for a long time and I want you to feel comfortable around me. I'll be here if you need me. . . if you need me for anything."

Sydney slowly extended her hand. "Friends then," she said as she reached out to shake Drew's hand. But it didn't feel like just friends. Their fingers touched, slid down each other's palms, and electricity melded their hands together. Still flushed from their encounter on the floor, their handshake lingered much too long, a sensuous caress vibrating between their palms. The heat of that exchange traveled through her body and made Sydney blush. Drew felt it too and slowly withdrew his hand, his fingers lightly touching her palm all the way to her fingertips before he let go. Their eyes locked. His body ached. All he wanted to do was take her into his arms and hold her, feel her body next to his and smother her in long, lustful kisses. But he also wanted to reaffirm that he respected her and didn't want to scare her away.

He flashed a warm smile. "I'll see you at dinner tonight. Save me a place next to you."

Sydney could feel her heart beat. "Are you sure you'll be back in time for dinner? It sounds like you have a pretty heavy workload at the clinic."

"I'll make it work," he said, not taking his eyes away from her.

"Dinner then. . .friend," she said, and quickly turned to walk away. She knew she needed to leave before her legs gave way beneath her. One year? Who was she kidding? Certainly not Drew. He diagnosed her. . .them. . .in an instant. He didn't have to be a doctor to read the chemistry levels between them. There was only one prescription for these symptoms. Sydney knew, and so did Drew.

eight

THE CHANGING TIDES

Two weeks in the jungle may sound like a long time, but the days flew by quickly. Drew and Reagan were kept busy at the clinic in Esperanza and because of the demands on them, both doctors ended up staying in a small hut next to the clinic for a few nights to eliminate the long boat rides—precious hours that could be used helping the clinic staff with seemingly endless line of patients who were arriving for care. Word travels fast in the jungle when doctors are available.

Despite his advanced medical training, Drew couldn't help but notice the successful methods of the rural native nurses in treating tropical parasites and local infectious protozoans. He was getting an advanced seminar in tropical medicine from the simply educated, but profoundly experienced staff.

Sydney was well aware of the needs of the clinic and was pleased these two American doctors were so dedicated to their practice. Besides, it made it easier for her to focus on her own therapy. She knew if Drew were nearby she would want to be with him every minute of the day. She hadn't felt that strong about anyone in a long time—maybe since the early days of her marriage, and that was a long time ago. This was different than any relationship she had before. She wondered if it was because she was trying to set boundaries and focus on herself instead of a relationship. What you can't have, you sometimes want the most. Or was this finally the soulmate she had been longing for? How would she know?

Sydney filled her days with activity to try to keep her mind off Drew. She went to nearby Chino Village with the lodge guests and visited with her old friends of many years. Children she had seen when she first began traveling to the jungle were now young mothers with fat babies nursing at their breasts. She photographed in the villages, played with the children, and gave out gifts she had brought. She always came with an extra bag of useful items, practical things like wooden spoons, soap, dish towels, clothespins, darning needles, thread and scissors for the women. She brought fish line and hooks, jackknives, headlamps, flashlights and nylon rope for the men and boys. The girls appreciated hair supplies like headbands, pretty barrettes, hair clips and pony tail binders. When she could, she brought school supplies, clothing and flip flops for the children. Dental care, as well as bandaids and general medical supplies were often donated by a small hospital back home.

She always brought copies of the photographs she had taken the last time she visited. Everyone loved getting photos of themselves and often laughed at how much they, or their children had changed since the last set of pictures. She loved documenting their lives for them. Sometimes Sydney wondered if the villagers remembered her because she always brought gifts or because she came so often. Perhaps both. It didn't matter. She was always happy to be there and challenged herself to remember the names of some of the native women who greeted her.

Sydney joined in with the women as they prepared local plants and seeds for dying chambira and stilt palm that would be used in weaving beautiful baskets and jewelry. She had done this many times and always marveled at how the messy seeds of the achiote pod could be crushed and boiled to make a rich red dye. Yellow color came from ginger root; black from huito fruit and shades of purple from mischqu panga seeds, with color combinations in between depending on how long the mixture was boiled on a crude wood fire on the dirt floor of the grass hut. This art center doubled as a market on Thursday when tourists from the lodge arrived to purchase baskets, carvings, jewelry and other creations the natives made completely from jungle materials, seeds and palm. Each piece was a true gift and Sydney had many of these treasures in her home. Yet she knew she would continue to purchase more just to support these gifted women and children who, with the help of Dolly, the lodge owner, had formed an art collective to support their families and continue traditions into the next generations.

Even though Sydney's days were eventful, yet relaxing, she couldn't help but casually inquire each night to Dolly about how the two doctors were doing in Esperanza. Dolly and Sydney had become good friends through the past fifteen or so years since they met at the lodge. Sydney, although she thought she was being discrete, couldn't put anything past Dolly.

"I think you should change your plan," Dolly said to her one evening after dinner and the guests had retreated to their rooms for the night.

"What do you mean?" Sydney asked.

"I mean 'one year,' really Syd. Are you serious?" Dolly laughed.

Sydney walked to the corner of the screened dining room and opened an ice cooler on the floor, taking out two cold sodas. Drinks were "on your honor" here, so she made two slash marks after her name on the clipboard, opened the bottles with the anaconda bottle opener attached to the bamboo wall by a string, and handed a soda to Dolly.

"I'm trying not to be offended," Sydney replied with a grin.

"Just so you know, he asks Augusto about you almost every day, wondering if the 'guests' ever come to Esperanza."

"He? Who?" Sydney was being coy.

"You know full well who I am talking about. I think I know you pretty well after all these years of seeing you interact with your groups and I've never seen you like this before. Always on the lookout at dinner, checking the chalkboard itinerary for his name, asking seemingly innocent questions about how things are going at the clinic. Really, Syd, you're pretty obvious!" Dolly smiled at her. "As much as you love this place, I think it would be perfect for you to meet someone here who shares your passion for the jungle."

Sydney peeled at the Inca Cola label on her soda bottle. "Is that how it happens? When you least expect it. I came down here alone this time to sort things out, to uncomplicate my life and find myself again. So what the hell am I doing, thinking about this man all the time, a man who I've only talked to a few times. It's so ridiculous. I'm not a school girl."

Dolly handed her an envelope. "But it seems that you both have that high school crush and there is only one thing to do about it," Dolly informed her. "See it through. It may be just a fling. If so, enjoy it. You deserve it! But, if you walk away, how will you know if you might be throwing away the real thing. You've waited a long time to find that again. I'm just saying. . ."

". . .yeah, yeah. A year is a long time." Sydney finished Dolly's sentence. "What's this envelope?"

"Drew asked our boatman to give it to you." Dolly winked.

"I also thought I should tell you that there is a supply boat going to Esperanza tomorrow and there just may be room for a passenger. You could offer to help in the clinic for the day. You've done that before, so you know the routine, *if* you can keep your mind on the patient and not the doctor!   Y o u could also document the progress going on there. We've added to the facility since you were here last." Dolly added, "We've just competed an addition of solar power for electricity, and refrigeration for polio vaccines and snake antivenin. The boat leaves at 5 a.m., so come down for an early breakfast if you decide to go."

"Hmmm. I'll think on it," Sydney replied as she downed the rest of her soda.

"Bring your rain gear. We're supposed to be in for some more heavy rains tonight. It's been raining so much, I was hoping we'd have a little break. Our water levels are already unusually high for this time of year," Dolly noted as she quietly closed the screen door of the dining hall behind her to retire for the evening. "Goodnight Syd. See you bright and early in the morning."

Sydney opened the envelope as soon as she got comfortable inside her mosquito netted bed. It was simple, yet sweet, written on prescription note paper, scribbled in doctor's almost non-legible handwriting.

"Sydney Knight. Take two deep breaths and one big smile before bedtime. Follow with a large dose of thinking of me, thinking of you as we listen to the raindrops and jungle songs that surround us both. Doctor's orders. Looking forward to seeing you in a few days. Drew."

Sydney tucked Drew's "prescription" into her journal. She followed the doctor's instructions and took two deep breaths before she closed her eyes. Sounds of the jungle joined them in an odd sort of way and the thought of seeing him again indeed made her smile. She welcomed the sound of rain as she drifted off to sleep with the first heavy drops showering down on her thatched roof. Drew was thinking of her. . . school girl indeed.

~~~~~~~

It had been raining a lot since Sydney arrived, but it rains most every day in the jungle. It's the rainforest. There are only two seasons here—the wet season from about November to May, and the dry season from June through October. Temperatures are close to the same year round, ranging in the 80s and 90s. The only difference is in the rainy season, guests travel more by boat and have opportunities to canoe deeper into remote areas when waters level are high. The river is usually highest in May and lowest in October. During dry season, these same areas are accessible on foot and those who like to hike and explore the jungle floor can walk for miles.

Sydney had brought groups to the area during both seasons and although she had enjoyed hiking a lot when she was younger, she realized that now she preferred boating during the rainy season when they could get deeper into the jungle's secret lakes and alcoves. Daily rain showers released humidity from the air and cooled off the jungle, at least for a few hours before it built up and recycled all over again. Plus, there was a refreshing rhythm to the rain in the jungle. Everything came alive.

Whether it rained lightly and continuously for a few hours, or poured furiously for long minutes, the air was permeated with odors that released themselves into raindrops of fragrant flowers, plants and vines. Afterward, rays of shamanic sunlight, beamed conical paths through the treetops all the way to the jungle floor. Sydney likened it to a flashlight beam shining from high atop the canopy onto a stage of brilliant green fungi, ferns and plants, teaming with its own world of life that few people ever notice. A world within itself. A world of nature that Sydney loved for its simplicity and its complexity.

Sydney woke early to catch the boat to Esperanza and was greeted by Dolly in the darkness of the bamboo corridor. Dolly was heading to the staff dining hall where her crew waited for an important meeting. It was going to be one of those complex days.

"You may as well join us," Dolly took hold of her arm. "You're like part of our staff and might want to hear this. We have a serious change of plans."

Dolly's brother, Rolex, who was the lodge manager, stood in front of the staff.

"Two men from Chino Village came with their families during the night by canoe in the rain to tell us that the river banks are overflowing and caving in because of the hard rain. Homes on the edges of the banks have been evacuated and natives are taking their canoes of supplies and rafts with chickens, pigs and dogs deeper into the jungle to find higher ground. Some of the houses on taller stilts are OK so far and their owners are moving all their belongings into the rafters, hoping the rain will stop and water will recede. Villages beyond Chino, like San Pedro have already been evacuated."

Rolex looked like he hadn't slept a wink all night. Taut lines tightened on his face. Some of his staff who lived in Chino had already headed to the village to save their families. The riverbank along the settlement was at least 15 to 20 feet high, so for it to have reached flood stage so quickly was serious. Plus, it was near the bend of the river, which meant that flood water making that turn would become forceful.

This kind of flooding is no stranger to the Amazon and it's to be taken more serious each year. In some parts of the rainforest logging continues to cause erosion. It's a domino effect. Those who gain monetarily from cutting down trees are changing the eco system of the rain forest and are not concerned with the consequences that affect villages along the smaller tributaries of the Amazon River. But flooding in the Tahuayo region is mainly caused from record hot summers in Peru's distant Andean mountains, where ancient, massive glaciers suddenly release incredible volumes of water that floods into the lower Amazon with little warning.

Floods can be devastating and several deaths occur each year from drowning during these floods, particularly among children. It's a very dangerous business, not only because of drowning hazards, but also from caiman, snakes, river rats, spiders, poisonous frogs, poisonous ants, and other species that will try to latch on to whatever they can to stand their ground, which just may be an occupied native hut or a human. Ground mammals like jaguar, puma, ocelot, tapir, and giant anteaters instinctively head to higher ground, but are also known to take refuge wherever they can. It's not a good situation.

"We're gathering tarps, blankets, buckets, medical supplies and food and heading to the village this morning. If the current isn't too strong, we'll see if we can transport children and the elderly back here where it'll be safer. Our lodge should be all right being we're on higher ground and built on taller stilts, but we'll be monitoring our safety here also. We don't want to alarm our guests, but will give them the option to head back to Iquitos if they feel threatened. Other than the transport boat for Iquitos, we'll need every boat we have to route to Chino to bring supplies to those who want to head deeper into the jungle to find higher ground. We'll also need to bring back villagers who want shelter here."

Rolex glanced at Sydney. "I'm here for the long run," she quickly said. "Tell me what I can do to help. Anything."

He nodded, knowing he could count on her. She knew the routine here after all these years and would be good helping to keep the guests calm. Luckily they had a small group this week. Out of the fifteen cabins at the lodge, the four college boys were in one cabin; the six senior citizens took up three cabins; the two doctors shared a cabin, and Sydney was in one cabin, so there would be ten double and triple rooms of extra lodging available for the villagers, plus the hammock room, which hung nine hammocks from the center out, like spokes on a wheel. If need be, there was also the lab, staff rooms, reading room and even the dining room. They would find places for everyone.

"When the breakfast drum bangs, I'd like you, Sydney, to be available when I break the news to our guests. If any of them want to return, help Bichina and the staff with their belongings so we can get them out of here as soon as possible. It's eight hours round trip to Iquitos, so the sooner we get our boat back the better. We'll need it," Dolly said. "Plus, we have a limited housekeeping staff because of our small group, so I may need help getting the cabins ready for villagers, if you and any volunteer guests can assist with that."

Sydney nodded.

Dolly quickly added, "And we have our boat coming from Esperanza with help and some supplies. Like us, they haven't been affected as much by the high water, so let's send out a prayer that continues."

Sydney understood she was referring to the two doctors, but honestly, Drew was farthest from her mind at this moment. She had so many native friends in Chino and was more concerned about their safety. Especially the children.

It didn't surprise anyone that none of the guests wanted to leave. They, too, were concerned for the villagers and wanted to assist in any way they could. Dolly and her small staff appreciated it as the college boys and senior citizens helped set up bedding, prepared extra food, got medical supplies ready, and kept things organized. Blankets, tarps and other supplies were loaded on boats that headed to Chino.

Dolly was reluctant to allow any of the guests to go to the village. It was too dangerous, but, as the day wore on, seeing that Bichina and her staff had everything under control at the lodge, Sydney insisted. She thought she could be of more help there, assisting her native friends to collect their things and get them loaded on the boats. It must be overwhelming for them. It was already late afternoon by the time she collected life jackets that had been worn by villagers who had already been brought to the lodge, and carried them to the boat to be reused by others who needed rescuing. She, herself, refused to wear one, knowing it might mean saving the life of a child or another person in the village. She braced herself, traveling head on into disaster.

~ nine ~

THE RESCUE

Mayhem met the crew even before they reached the village. Families in dugout canoes were stranded alongside the high river banks, holding on to tree branches for dear life, trying not to capsize in the fast current. Everyone was bailing water as fast as they could, using rusty aluminum cans and plastic buckets. Rolex's Tahuayo Lodge boat headed over to collect the canoers, filling their boat with drenched villagers, and then turned around to return to the lodge with their load of survivors. Lodge guides tied the extra canoes behind the speedboats that continued on to the village. They would have to sort out later who were the owners. It takes months to make a dugout canoe and, next to their machete, it was the most important possession for survival in the jungle that a family owned. For now, every vessel was needed.

The pace was just as frantic in the village as the speedboats pulled up next to rafters of thatched roof huts that had been built on stilts more than 20 feet above the waterline. People were hanging on to the highest beams in their homes, waving for the boats to rescue them. Some already had rafts filled with supplies and were attempting to maneuver further into the jungle to reach higher ground. The dugout canoes were quickly filled with tarps and supplies the lodge had brought and natives hurriedly paddled through the trees, searching for safety. The sky was dark from the heavy rain with black clouds overhead. Flashlight beams signaled a trail of rescue workers, illuminated by occasional flashes of lightning.

Sydney helped hand out supplies to those who were hoping to find refuge deeper in the jungle, mostly the men of the village who had sent their women, children and elders into the speedboats headed back to the lodge. The boats would continue back and forth into the evening if necessary until everyone was rescued. Some of the men refused to leave. They had been through floods before and would ride it out to protect their animals. Men sat atop the thatch of their roof, with their canoe tied nearby, determined to stay as long as they could. Pigs, chickens, and goats were securely tied to the roof. Dogs barked, their frantic yelps swallowed by the roar of raging water.

Sydney helped a crying child aboard the crowded boat and seeing there was no room for her, she waved at the boatman to go. She could hear the motor of another boat coming back and would take it out with the others. Balancing on rafters of an abandoned thatched hut, she could see lodge staff helping other villagers get ready for the boat's return. She hadn't thought out a strategy and now realized that she, too, was stranded until another boat arrived. The last thing she wanted was for herself to have to be rescued, or worse yet, become a victim of the fierce floodwaters.

As Sydney shifted her weight to get a little higher off the rising water she could feel the swaying of the stilts that held up the hut. Suddenly the rafters beneath Sydney broke loose and she plummeted into the swirling water below. Sydney tried to grip the thatch above her, but the current was too strong. She grasped desperately at a chunk of rafter boards and pulled herself onto the rough wood. Laying flat on her stomach, she held tight to the make-shift raft, screaming as the swirling water carried her away from the ruined hut.

It was only minutes, but seemed like hours as she crashed through the waves of dirty river water on her wooden raft. She closed her eyes and had a quick flashback of a time when she was about six years old. Her family had just arrived back from town in a dark, threatening rain storm. It began to hail. Hard, golf-ball size hail, the kind that could cause serious injury. They waited in the car for it to stop but it wasn't letting up. Sydney's parents and baby brother were in the front seat, with Sydney and her older brother in the back.

"I can make it stop," an innocent Sydney confidently announced, noticing the concern of her parents. She closed her eyes and concentrated. . .and the hail suddenly stopped. Her mom held the baby close and scrambled with her dad to the porch. It happened so quickly that Sydney and her brother just sat in the back seat and watched their parents rush to the house. As soon as they were safe, the hail started again. Her parents were distraught seeing the two children hadn't followed them.

Sydney's brother looked at her and said, "Bet you can't do it again." With that, she closed her eyes and concentrated. The hail stopped again and they ran to the house.

"I did it! I did it!" Sydney exclaimed as they reached the porch just in time for the sky to unleash another burst of hail.

"Don't be silly. It was just a coincidence," her dad said as he hustled them inside the house. But little Sydney knew better. She knew she had made a miracle. Twice.

Sydney wondered for a brief moment if she could stop this storm, if that power was still somewhere inside her. Before she could try, her raft bumped against a large branch coursing down the river and she had all she could do to hold on to the splintered boards that were keeping her afloat.

Through the loud rushing of the river she thought she could faintly hear the motor of a boat getting louder and knew it was nearing. Sydney prayed the boatman would be able to intercept her, but the current was too strong. She screamed again as her raft bumped hard against the rescue boat, almost plummeting her into the water, and then swiftly began to swerve away, toward the opposite side of the raging river. She felt a loud thump and closed her eyes, sending up a prayer, "Oh God, please don't let me die like this. Please help me. Please."

Sydney's heart jumped a beat as she felt something fall on top of her and cover her body. "Oh, God," she cried, thinking of giant anacondas or frightened jaguars falling from the trees above.

"It's OK. It's OK. I'm here," Drew shouted as he shielded her weary body from the low branches of a tree.

Sydney opened her eyes in disbelief. "Where....how....?" she began, realizing that he must have jumped from the boat as it passed by her makeshift raft.

"Hang on," was Drew's only response as he attempted to grab hold of low lying branches on the edge of the riverbank to inch them toward terra firme, avoiding a large black palm with dozens of six-inch spines. He managed to maneuver the floorboard raft through the fast current, and using branches for leverage, he finally wedged the narrow craft between two trees, docking it high enough and tight enough to release it from the water's mighty grip. Sydney's body lay limp from exhaustion, her hands bloodied from her grip. She didn't move.

Drew quickly rolled her over to see if she was alive. She flung her arms around him and sobbed. The rain beat down on them, but she felt safe in Drew's arms. He held her. The sky was still black from dark clouds and pouring rain, with only flashes of lighting illuminating them.

"I can't believe this is happening," she cried.

"Are you all right?" the doctor in him asked, holding her at arms length, checking her over.

"I. . .I think so," she stuttered. "I don't know. I'm alive."

Lightning flashed again and the thin cotton of Sydney's blouse clung to her breasts, outlining her body as she shivered in the cold rain. Drew grabbed her and held her close to keep her warm. He could feel her taut nipples against his open shirted bare chest. Unexpectedly, in the wrath of the storm, their lips met in frantic, lustful kisses. Adrenaline flowed through their bodies and released itself in a passion that neither of them could control. His mouth moved down her neck onto her breasts. Massaging her fingers through his thick wet hair, Sydney encouraged his bold enthusiasm. His hands moved down her body, caressing her while pressing his manhood tight against her. They may as well have been naked, as their soaking wet clothing clung to their bodies, highlighting every curve and crevice. Streaks of lightning and sheets of rain heightened their desire.

Drew knew this was obsessive, but logic didn't play into his naked emotion. The danger of the raging elements around them only intensified the fervor of their kisses. Sydney, too, knew this was insane. They could die, right here and now in this turbulent river. It was a good way to die, she surmised—engulfed in the passion they both felt. She wanted this man. She wanted him mind, soul and body, and right now, his body was so boldly meshed with hers that she didn't care about an outcome. Even death.

Abruptly, before they could go any further, they were jolted out of their blind obsession and thrown back into treacherous reality as their makeshift raft began to let loose from its perch. At the same time they heard a voice shouting from the darkness beyond.

"Doctor Harris! Miss Sydney! Can you hear me?"

A beam of light from one of the rescue boats flashed off and on into the sky, signaling that the lodge guides had come back to rescue them.

"Hello," the frantic voice shouted into the abyss. "Doctor Harris. Miss Sydney. Are you there?"

Drew raised himself up and grabbed a branch to steady their raft. Keeping one arm around Sydney to keep her close, he attempted to regain his senses.

"Whew," Sydney let out a heaving sigh.

"Hang on to me," Drew said. Sydney clung to him. She wasn't about to let go.

"Over here," Drew yelled into the dark. "Over here," he shouted, waving his arms in another flash of lightning. "Over here. We're OK. We're both OK."

Rolex followed Drew's voice and expertly maneuvered the boat to retrieve them from their tree perch. The boat was overloaded with the last of the villagers. Drew and Sydney were wedged close together between the others and given a pancho to cover their wet, shivering bodies—but it was not the violent rain or even the chill of the storm that made their bodies tremble. Sydney closed her eyes and laid her head on Drew's chest as he put his arm around her to keep her near. She was safe. She also knew it would be a very short year.

~~~~~

Sydney was relieved to finally see the lanterns of the lodge as they rounded the bend. The boat was quickly emptied as everyone hurried to take refuge from the pouring rain. Sydney was exhausted and headed straight to her room for a shower to warm her aching bones. Even a tepid shower would feel good. She looked out her screen window and stood for a moment, watching the thin strands of lightning continue to flash their way across the river, silhouetting the jungle canopy. She always thought lightning was fascinating.

She remembered as a young girl when she went outside with her dad late one afternoon to watch an approaching storm. They lived in the Midwest and her dad was farming at the time. Weather could be his best friend or his worst enemy. Suddenly a bolt of lightning struck a huge oak tree that was only about 50 feet from them. Sydney's dad fell to the ground and she remembered her mother running to him and practically carrying him to the door. She frantically called for Sydney to get into the house. But Sydney just stood there, her white sundress and long blonde hair blowing in the wind as she watched lightning dance through the sky. A large branch on the oak tree split open and crashed to the ground, hanging onto its trunk with white threads of splinters that were soon devoured in flames. Fire came from inside the tree, as if it had finally escaped its dungeon and bellowed out like a dragon, reaching for the sky, throwing balls of flames all around. Then the rain came and swiftly drowned the fire back into its den, leaving only charred black footprints on the trunk. Sydney stood mesmerized until her mother finally pulled her into the safety of the house.

Oddly enough, Sydney was never afraid of storms after that. She was always in awe of the power of nature—of lightning, fire, rain, and respected its forceful energy, but after tonight, she hoped she would never experience another close encounter with nature's dominance.

Drew carried a small child into the dining hall and helped the weary mother. They were quickly escorted to a room where they could get dry clothes and warm beds. Reagan was on duty, helping the lodge staff check on new arrivals. He assured Drew that they had it under control.

"You look like hell," Reagan said. "Get some warm clothes—and then get some sleep."

Drew didn't linger. The day had gone by fast and night was approaching. He had another patient he needed to check on after his shower.

No one locks their doors in the jungle lodge. It's safe. So when Sydney heard a knock on the door, followed by the turning of the knob, she wasn't alarmed.

"Sydney," Drew called before he cracked open the door. "Are you OK? Can I come in?"

Sydney shuddered as the rain continued to pound on the thatched roof of her cabin. She was glad to hear Drew's voice.

"I didn't know doctors made house calls anymore," she said as she wrapped her robe around her while attempting to dry her hair with a towel.

"This is an exception."

Drew stepped inside, closing the door behind him.

"I saw you limping when you got off the boat and thought I should check on you."

Sydney tried to hide it, but the truth was that she was bruised all over and had a lot of pain in her ankle. She may have bumped it against a branch or twisted it trying to stay afloat on the raft. Her body still felt shaken by the ordeal—nearly drowning AND the boldness of their passion. She admitted her injury and sat down on the bed to take her weight off it.

Drew sat on the bed next to her and gently lifted her ankle onto his lap. It was bruised and starting to swell. He wanted to take precautions.

"Does this hurt?" he questioned as he gently moved her foot.

Sydney winced. "Just a little," she said, trying to be brave as he examined her ankle, feeling for broken bones.

"I don't think anything is broken, but you may have a nasty sprain. You'll need to keep it elevated and stay off it for a few days. We'll have to get some ice for it and I'll keep an eye on that swelling." He carefully wrapped her ankle in a bandage that he retrieved from his doctor bag. "And you must keep under the watchful eye of your doctor to avoid complications," he grinned.

"I think it's too late for that," Sydney responded. "Avoiding complications."

Their eyes locked.

"Yeah. That was pretty intense. I hope I wasn't out of line," he retreated.

"Only if I was," she boldly replied.

Drew's fingers slowly massaged their way up her calf. "Maybe I should check to be sure there aren't any other injuries."

Sydney realized that she couldn't deny her desire when it came to this man. Surprising herself, she aggressively leaned toward him and bared her shoulder.

"I have a little bruise here," she expressed, lowering her robe to suggest her nakedness beneath. "Maybe you should do a more thorough examination, Doctor."

"Oh, I can see that shoulder will need some real attention," Drew said, not wasting any time. His fingers traced the lines of her collar bone. "There is definitely a need for some therapy here," he said as his lips lightly brushed her neck, working down her tan shoulder to the roundness of her flesh. Sydney embraced him to her bosom, sinking her fingers into his unruly, damp hair, encouraging his attention.

Drew slowly pushed her back on the bed, gently caressing her supple body. Their lips met in frantic kisses. Sydney responded with a sigh as she massaged her hands down the hard muscles of his back. Drew reacted to her sensuousness as his lips caressed her breasts, his tongue moving slowly down to her belly. His hands reached inside her robe, following down each curve to fondle the softness of her body. Sydney let her robe fall away and opened to the foreplay of his touch. His lips lightly brushed the insides of her legs and she responded with longing moans to his tenderness. His seduction made her senses go wild. She closed her eyes to delight in all the pleasures and intuitively responded to Drew's lovemaking. She didn't want to think. She just wanted to feel. She wanted this man to be lost in her. Coaxed on by her hunger, Drew reached for the small of her back and raised her to meet the throbbing tightness of his body. Drew's tender lovemaking soon turned into arousing intensity and their kisses were met with an outburst of uncontrollable passion as they moved together in a rhythm of sexual pleasure. They were overcome by the fever of their desire, as flares of lightning outlined their joined bodies and the lust that had engulfed them on the river resumed through the night with no one to interrupt their seductive appetite for each other.

~~~~~

"Thank you," Sydney said the next morning as she rolled over, connecting with Drew's sleepy eyes.

"Thank you?" he grinned. "That's an interesting response after an intense night of lovemaking."

"Seriously," Sydney was solemn as she snuggled into his arms. "I mean thank you for saving my life. If you hadn't done your stuntman leap onto my raft and wedged us between those trees, I probably wouldn't be here today. I still don't know how you did it."

"Honestly, I don't know either. There certainly was a higher power out there working last night. Believe me, I'm just as grateful as you. I think a lot of folks here will have miracle stories that pulled them through last night. I just hope there aren't any serious injuries or worse."

"Thank God Reagan was here to tend to everyone while you were out playing Indiana Jones!"

"And thank God for you, Sydney. I think you've also saved me."

Before she could respond, Sydney heard a knock on her door.

"Syd. I heard about last night. Are you all right?" Dolly asked.

"Yes, I'm fine. I'll be out in half an hour," Sydney responded. "I want to hear about the damages from last night—to see if there is anything I can do to help."

"See you at breakfast," Dolly called out, as she walked away.

"Half an hour?" Drew questioned. "I was hoping for more time with you this morning," he hinted, nuzzling her neck. "I see a few more bruises that may need attention. And didn't I tell you to stay off that ankle? I think bed rest is the only solution."

"I'll be fine. I'll get a walking stick from Bichina and stay off my foot as much as I can. As much as I'd love to stay and have you attend to *all* my needs, I think there'll be much use for a doctor this morning in the village," Sydney replied, gently kissing his lips.

Drew responded to her kiss with his tongue outlining the inner flesh of her mouth, coaxing her back into his arms. She yielded to his touch and they again made love with as much enthusiasm as the night before, trying hard to keep their heavy breathing and moans of passion from echoing through the thin walls of the cabin, into the daylight beyond. Today, there was no rain to drown out the sounds of the ecstasy of their lovemaking.

Finally, Sydney sighed, as they lay exhausted on the bed, spent from their desire. They could hear the shuffle of feet and the boardwalk creaking as people rushed by. Voices chattered excitedly and oars banged on the sides of boats being readied to assess the damage in the village.

"There won't be much privacy with my room so close to the dining hall," she said as she gently traced the lines of a deep cut on his forehead. He had wounds from the storm too.

"You should have a doctor take a look at this so it doesn't get infected."

"I know. I'll take care of it," he said, knowing that doctors are the worst patients.

Sydney laughed. "Your cut looks like a lightning bolt. I think it may just leave a scar. Very Harry Potter-ish."

"I hope it does," Drew smiled. "Then every time I look at it in the mirror, I'll be reminded of this stormy, lightning-filled night and the electricity of our first night together."

Sydney softly kissed his injury. "A wound is the place where light enters you," she quoted Rumi.

"Then my wounds are open to the world," Drew replied. "I welcome that light. . . your light, Sydney. Now that I have a taste, I don't think I can get enough of you."

Sydney smiled. From where did this charming man come? She felt so blessed that she had fallen into his arms when she had least expected it. Indeed, the Universe works in mysterious ways.

ten

ÆFTER THE STORM

The sun shone brightly through thick jungle and the calm river reflected white billowing clouds above as if nothing had happened during the stormy night. But nature's fury was still evident with trees and debris that had twisted themselves along the edges of the river banks. Dolly didn't want her guests to feel they were obligated to help in the villages, but she understood how travelers receive a sense of satisfaction doing whatever they can to help. Often giving was more gratifying than receiving. There was a lot that needed to be done. Everyone was eager to help.

Navigating from the lodge to Chino Village was difficult that first morning, as the course of the river had changed. The raging water dug new tributaries through the jungle and old passages were cluttered with fallen trees. Monkeys chattered loudly and swung from high branches, accessing their new unfamiliar landscape. The usually cheerful lodge staff and river guides were somber. Everything was muddy.

The storm had taken its toll on many levels. One of the elderly men, Moycon, had died trying to save his livestock. His son found him floating on the debris of water next to his hut. Moycon had tied his animals to the top of his roof to keep them from falling into the water, but he had fallen into the turbulent river while trying to retrieve another animal that was being whisked away in the current. A rope that had tangled around the man's ankle kept him from floating down river in the wreckage. They surmised that he had hit his head when he fell, which knocked him unconscious before he drowned. His dog barked furiously, pulling at the rope, trying to save his master. Two pigs on top of the hut squealed, hens in a roughly made wooden cage squawked, and a goat just stood there, eating thatch from the top of the roof, oblivious to his surroundings.

Moycon's family—his wife, children and grandchildren along with the entire community, was grieving the loss of this good man. This was a hard time and burial arrangements were made immediately so people could begin the process of rebuilding of their homes. For them, it meant survival.

A few guests were curious about the procedure of funerals in the jungle, so Dolly had explained that there was a cemetery behind the village, a distance away from the huts. She hoped it hadn't been disturbed by the flood waters. When someone in the village died, loved ones would clean the dead body and dress it with a favorite outfit of the deceased. If they were wearing rings or any ornament on the body, or had metal in their teeth, like gold crowns or fillings, the family would remove it.

"Older people believe that metal burns the dead body, but also gold is valuable," she stated. "The body is wrapped with a sheet and placed on a table over another sheet, and a candle or kerosene lamp is placed on all four corners of the table. Close relatives wear black and family and friends pay their respects, visiting the dead. At night, usually around 1 a.m., the family serves coffee, bread and butter, and chicken soup. To pass the time, people play bingo and some men play cards."

Dolly smiled at the reaction of her guests at the comment of mourners playing games. "They have to find something to pass the time because the body is kept there for 24 hours before it's taken to the cemetery. At the gravesite someone, usually the shaman, says a prayer, and people cry out memories of their dead loved one. The body is then placed in a wooden box and put into the ground. Cremation isn't usually practiced here," she added.

But this burial was going to be different. Moycon's wife, Xina, said that Moycon had told them many times that when he died he wanted to be buried in the tradition of his tribe, the Achuar, from the Huagramona region of the Amazon. He wanted to follow them into the spirit world in the old ways of his people. He wanted to be cremated. And so it was.

As soon as the water levels had receded and the 24 hour visitation was complete, villagers gathered around the family. The body of Moycon had been wrapped in dried palm tree fronds and placed inside his dugout canoe. Everyone, young and old, took turns stepping forward to pay tribute by telling a story about him, or just saying thank you to this man who had been a generous neighbor, good friend, and favorite grandfather in the community. It was a touching "goodbye" as the wind carried these words of praise and gratitude into the canoe and wrapped them around the body so he would know their love. Then his oldest son paddled a canoe out onto the river, pulling his father's coffin canoe along side. He dropped a weight to anchor Moycon's canoe in place and then solemnly set fire to the dried palm before slowly paddling away. Agony wrenched at his face as he fought to hold back his sorrow and be a brave son.

The village cried. Dolly and her staff cried. He had been a great friend.

And Sydney cried. She had known this man. She knew his family. He had carved a walking stick for her the first time she came to the jungle to help her maneuver through terrain, and when she returned to the village the next time, he proudly showed her the t-shirt she had given him the year before. It had a peace symbol and Woodstock, NY printed on the front. He remembered her. His wife and daughter-in-law had made two of the beautiful woven baskets she treasured. She had held one of Moycon's newborn grandchildren in her arms when the baby was just weeks old. They felt like family.

Everyone watched as Moycon's body burned, flames extending into the sky, smoke fusing with white billowy clouds, reaching into the world of ancestors. Tears turned to silence when the fiery flames finally sank the charred canoe. The ashes and bones of Moycon disappeared into the deep, dark waters of the river. Whatever else remained would be an offering to nature, to the creatures of the river. It was a somber day and, other than cooking to feed the community gathered, much of the work had stopped for the hours of the burning in respect for the family.

"Sometimes, in a traditional burial for an Achuar head of household where Moycon's ancestors came from, the body is placed in the canoe and is buried in the middle of the house in remembrance of their presence," Dolly explained. "That way, body parts are able to acquire another life and can assume the bodies of certain animals to protect the family. It's the same with ashes and remaining bones in a river burial."

Drew and Reagan had never seen anything like this before and were taken aback by the honesty of the ceremony. They too shed tears and wished they had known the man Moycon.

~~~~~

The next few days were a whirlwind of activity. Cleaning and restoring huts that had survived to provide shelter for as many families as possible was high on the repair list. Rebuilding lost huts from scratch involved going out into the jungle and cutting down selected trees for structure, flooring and furniture. Large palm fronds needed to be cut and woven into thatch for new roofs, and there was a never ending search for lost pigs, goats, chickens, dogs and dugout canoes. The Tahuayo Lodge prepared meals and guests helped distribute them to the village. Small children were brought to the lodge to be looked after while their parents went about reconstructing their homes.

Villager's lives were normally simple. Most owned one or two cooking pots, scant utensils, hammocks, blankets, some clothing, fishing gear and most important, a machete and a dugout canoe. Those who lost everything had to start from scratch and there were no stores around to replenish anything. They relied on each other and Tahuayo Amazonia Lodge, who had always been generous to help support the community.

Maria, the village herbalist had lost her entire herb garden in the flood. All of the precious plants she had searched out, carefully dug up deep within the jungle, transported back and replanted, were washed away. Even herbal plants drying on the beams of her thatched hut were gone. All of her healing knowledge would help care for the injured, but she would have to replant her jungle pharmacy from scratch. She helped Drew and Reagan when they went to assess the many injuries. They bandaged cuts and scratches, removed nasty wood splinters, stitched up a few deep gashes and treated some sprained limbs.

Sydney volunteered to assist the doctors and she and Drew managed a few conversations and suggestive eye contact during these busy days. Just being near each other, brushing against each other, and knowing the feelings were mutual was alluring. But each night, back at the lodge, their lovemaking feverishly burned as their bodies intertwined and heaved with passion until they lay exhausted, with only a few hours of sleep before they headed back to help Chino reclaim her river banks and redefine village life.

Each morning Sydney was greeted by the mirthful smiles and giggles of the native women who worked at the lodge. At first she wondered why they whispered to each other and grinned at her, until Dolly informed her that they always know when people at the lodge are making love. The buildings shake and noises are easily perceptible to the finely tuned ears of the natives. Sydney was embarrassed, yet she respected the native people's resilience, even good humor in the face of disaster.

~~~~~

"I'm heading deeper into the jungle today to dig some herbs to help Maria replenish her stock," Augusto said to Sydney early one morning. "I thought you and the Docs might like to go with me. It would be a good chance for them to check out our pharmacy."

Augusto, an Amazonia Expeditions guide for many years, was assigned to the doctors as their jungle guide. He was born in Chino Village and as a child, the forests of the Tahuayo were his playground. After elementary school in Chino and high school in Iquitos, he specialized in English studies in Iquitos and Lima. Augusto worked for several years as a research field assistant with Wildlife Conservation Society scientists before coming to work at the Tahuayo lodge. His specialties as a guide included wildlife tracking, birding and jungle survival training. He was also an expert in plants.

Knowing that restocking the local herbal "pharmacy" was important for the welfare of the villagers, Sydney, Drew and Reagan agreed to the adventure. They soon found themselves traveling into areas that tourists seldom venture. The boat ride itself was exciting. Augusto and their boatman, Ricardo, pointed out several species of monkeys, including the illusive bald-headed Red Uakari monkey that is only found in this region of the Amazon. They saw a mother sloth and her baby high in a tree where wild blue and yellow macaw were perched. At one point Reagan started to reach up to grasp a tree branch to use for leverage to help push the boat through a narrow channel. Augusto grabbed his arm just in time to stop him and then pointed to a tree boa that was coiled around the branch, inches from Reagan's hand. Reagan quickly retreated to his seat. "Don't worry, it's not poisonous," Augusto reported. "But if it bit you, it would be painful."

Ricardo spotted a small bird on a branch and maneuvered the boat underneath it. He whistled a hoarse tune that seemed to hypnotize the bird. Slipping his finger underneath the mesmerized bird's feet, he removed it from its perch and brought it over to Sydney, telling her to pet its head. The bird seemed to be sleeping as she gently stroked its gray feathers. Ricardo continued his soft whistles until he replaced the bird carefully on the branch. As soon as he stopped whistling, the bird opened its eyes and flew away. Jungle magic.

Drew and Reagan were equally impressed when Augusto aimed a crude, handmade spear toward a spot in the black water of the river. Both men strained their eyes, but couldn't see anything, no movement underneath, not even bubbles or tiny waves. Reagan teased him about pulling their leg, until Augusto let go of his spear and came up with a fish—an arapaima that was at least 20 inches long.

"Wow!" Reagan exclaimed.

"It's just a baby," Augusto said, holding up his spear so the fish's large blackish-green scales and red markings shone in the sunlight. "These are endangered species and protected by law," he said as he released the fish back into the dark waters and watched it swim away.

He added, "Arapaima are among the largest freshwater fish in the world. The biggest one on record was 15 feet long. You don't see many of them anymore, but we caught one here a few years ago that was over six feet long. It almost capsized our boat."

"Now you're really pulling my leg," Reagan said.

Augusto just smiled.

"It's true," Ricardo backed him up. "The arapaima are our river monsters."

Reagan decided he would no longer take his daily swims in the river at the lodge.

Augusto continued to spear fish and caught several vampire fish and butterfly peacock bass. He put them in a bucket of water to keep them fresh. They would enjoy an evening meal of tasty fish tonight.

Finally they arrived at their destination. After a short hike through dense terrain, with the guides using their machetes to chop the way, Sydney was surprised to see a small waterfall cascading from higher ground. She hadn't known there were waterfalls in this area.

Augusto noted her reaction. "Now you know why I thought you might like to tag along on this trip."

"You were right! This is such a discovery. Is it OK to swim here?" she asked, eyeing the inviting pool below the spill of the falls, and raising her camera to record this new place.

"As safe as it is to swim in the river," he answered, which really didn't give her much confidence. "If you stay close to the cascade, you should be safe. I swim here whenever I come to harvest plants."

Ricardo had already gathered their pails and bags for collecting. Reagan, who had always been an avid gardener was anxious to help. Drew had other thoughts, reading Sydney's playful glance.

"You guys go on ahead. I'll stay here and guard Sydney from river monsters. The buddy system is always safer."

The other three men chuckled as they headed toward an overgrown path with Augusto leading, chopping the way with his machete. "We'll be back in an hour," he shouted over his shoulder. "Here's an extra machete if you need it." He stabbed it into a nearby log. "Never go into the jungle without a machete."

Sydney nodded, taking off her boots and socks to test the water with her toe.

"Are you up for a swim?" she asked, looking over her shoulder to be sure the men had disappeared down the path before removing her clothes and wading into the dark water. Her tan skin rippled with goosebumps as cold water swirled around her.

"I am now," he responded, removing his clothing and following her, naked, into the chilly river. "Oh yeah. I'm up for it."

Sydney swam under the spray of the falls and let refreshing drops of water fall over her body. A small stream of sunlight found its way through the jungle canopy and highlighted her firm breasts. She didn't know how beautiful she looked at that moment—wet and deliciously tempting. But Drew knew. He quickly swam over to join her.

"Isn't this great," she shouted above the roar of the waterfall, shaking the water from her hair.

"It's amazing," he said, his eyes devouring her body. "Beautiful." He reached for her.

Sydney playfully splashed him with water.

"Oh, you want to play that way," he laughed, splashing back at her, initiating a serious water fight.

Their playfulness heightened the sexual excitement in the air and finally Drew pulled Sydney's naked body next to his. He felt her legs go tight around his hips. Their lips met and tongues entwined into each other's yielding mouths. Drew eagerly fondled Sydney's breasts, sending shivers down her spine. They braced themselves against the trunk of a fallen ceiba tree that was partially laying under the water. Drew's mouth found droplets from the waterfall's spray on Sydney's neck and shoulders and eagerly swallowed them, inch by inch, with his tongue licking and tasting the wet surface of her smooth skin. She sighed, breathing heavily as her tongue gently outlined his earlobe and explored the crevices of his ear. This drove Drew mad with an outburst of wild passion and soon Sydney felt his hands wander to her firm buttocks as he lifted and pulled her into him. She spun her body to willingly accommodate his manly thrusts and they moved in rhythm together, to the accompanying roar of the waterfall splashing cooling water onto their yielding bodies. The only thing they heard was their own moans of lustful desire being fulfilled, echoing into the depths of the jungle around them as they pulsed and throbbed within each other. When their heights had been reached, they clung to each other, breathing heavily, their fiery ardor turning to tender emotion. Drew brushed the wet hair from Sydney's face and kissed her gently, sweetly.

"You're amazing," he said, their naked bodies still rubbing and caressing each other's skin in the coolness of the river.

"I was going to say the same thing about you," she cooed.

They swam together to the river bank and slowly dried each other, caressing and embracing as they dressed, slowly buttoning each others shirts.

Suddenly Sydney gasped and told Drew not to move.

"Wha...." he started, and then noticed a huge gray tarantula clinging to the side of his sleeve.

"Don't move," she repeated. "If you don't show fear, it won't hurt you." She reached for a large leaf, the kind they used as hats or umbrellas to keep dry from the rain. Knowing that tarantulas can jump to three feet to catch their prey, she carefully coaxed the hairy spider to release its claws from the fabric of Drew's shirt.

Drew kept as still as possible. He knew that tarantulas were venomous and bites can range from serious discomfort to intense spasms over a period of several days, but none had been recorded as causing a human fatality. However, in his travels as a doctor, he had come across individuals who had severe allergic reactions from the venom's toxins, which could be life threatening. He didn't want to test out his allergic tolerance just now.

The creature gradually moved onto the leaf.

Sydney walked over and gently placed the leaf on a log.

"Go your way, Grandmother Spider," she whispered.

"I'm impressed," Drew let out a sigh of relief. "You were so calm."

"I've never been afraid of spiders," Sydney said. "Some cultures believe they represent the

Grandmother, the teacher and protector of esoteric wisdom. They're symbolic."

"I've never looked at them that way," the doctor admitted. "In my world, we'd either squash it, or dissect it for examination." He thought he was being clever. Sydney winced.

Drew noticed her frown and grabbed the machete. "Maybe we should see if we can find our way to this pharmacy of Augusto's," he changed the subject. "It should be easy to follow where they cut a path."

They followed the narrow, but defined, pathway through the jungle with Drew swinging the machete to trim more overgrowth, not necessarily because he had to, but because he liked the feeling of being a jungle warrior. Both had been in the jungle enough before to know what trees not to touch because of sharp, spiny needles or poisonous isula ants, and to watch for snakes—on the ground and in the trees.

They had walked for about ten minutes when all of a sudden they stopped in their tracks. They heard what they thought was a barking dog, but in the jungle you never know what sounds define an animal. The sound was coming closer. Sydney was several yards behind Drew, to keep out of the swath of his machete, and was about to take steps to catch up to him, when a small dog jumped into the path between them and barked, ferociously, jumping back and forth.

Sydney stopped and Drew rushed toward her, machete ready. The dog, now only a yard from Sydney, began to circle something in the trail, something that was almost under Sydney's foot. He plunged back and forth at it and then suddenly stopped and looked at each of them and then back at the spot in the trail a couple of times as if to say, "Stop! Look at this!"

It wasn't the dog they had to fear, but a giant toad, as big as basketball and Sydney was about to step right on it. Its camouflaged creamy color blended with the trail and she didn't even see it. Drew, in his long stride, had stepped right over it. They stood still, stunned that this dog was warning them to stay away. Drew cautiously stepped around the toad and the dog to join Sydney on the other side and they moved a few feet down the path, clear of the giant brown toad.

Suddenly they heard crashing noises coming down the path toward them. Drew stepped in front of Sydney, his machete raised. "What now?" he hoarsely whispered.

"Are you two OK," Augusto asked as he ran breathlessly toward them. "I thought I heard a dog barking."

Drew pointed to the toad.

"You're lucky," Augusto said immediately. "It's a cane toad. That thing is so poisonous. You'd have gone paralyzed instantly if you came in contact with its venom. That barking dog may have saved your life."

"Really?" Drew said, pulling Sydney close to him.

"Well, they are poisonous, but only if your mouth comes in contact with its venom," he smiled. "I don't think Sydney was planning on kissing any toads today."

Sydney laughed at his remark as she looked around for the dog that had saved them. It was gone.

"The dog just came out of nowhere," she exclaimed. "It was barking even before it got to us, as if it knew we were going to be in danger."

"If I hadn't heard it myself, I wouldn't have believed there could be a dog here. No one lives around here. Did it seem wild? Are you sure it was a dog?" Augusto questioned.

"It was a dog, small, brown and white. A mutt," Drew replied. "It didn't look wild. It stopped and looked at us to be sure we got his message. He warned us to stay away from that toad."

By then Ricardo and Reagan had caught up to the group. Augusto pointed to the toad and told them what had happened.

"Are you two OK?" Reagan was concerned. "You should have just waited for us at the waterfall."

But Ricardo was calm. He slowly smiled and said something to Augusto in Spanish. Augusto returned his smile and nodded.

"What? What did he say?" Reagan asked, still concerned for his friends.

"He said it was a spirit animal," Augusto repeated.

"It was the dog spirit of Moycon," Ricardo clarified. "You know, the man we buried. One of his power animals was a dog. You honored him at his burial, now his spirit shape-shifted to warn you of the danger."

Sydney smiled. She respected the spiritual and shamanic ways of indigenous people and felt honored that the jungle spirits were around her.

Drew and Reagan didn't know what to think. They just stared at each other and shrugged their shoulders. Animal spirits? Shape-shifting? It was beyond their scientific minds to comprehend.

~ eleven ~

JUNGLE FEVER

It had been a hectic week and guests had left the lodge to return home. Most of the staff had finished their shifts and returned to their families. A change of staff would arrive in a week with the next round of guests. The lodge was quiet with only Dolly, her lodge manager brother Rolex, her staff manager sister Bichina, a chef, housekeeper, and two guides remaining, along with Drew, Reagan and Sydney.

Dolly encouraged the trio to take at least a day break and go zip lining over the jungle canopy, or fishing. Sydney declined, thinking it would be good for the men to have their friend time. After all, they had traveled here to spend time together. She just happened to be a lucky circumstance. She needed to catch up on her journaling and really needed some down time. This idea of getting away to relax was not at all what she had in mind. Between her infatuation with Drew and the disaster in the village, she had found little time for herself. She was glad for the break. She headed to the hammock room.

~~~~~

In the village there was still much to be done. Fatigue was taking its toll.

Juan, a ten-year-old boy, had been doing more than his share to keep up to his elders as they worked day and night to make shelter for their family. After hard days of helping his father cut trees and haul heavy wood, he collapsed in the jungle, feverish and shaking. His father carried him to the home of Rosita, the local shaman woman, whose hut was on higher ground, deeper into the jungle and not as damaged from the heavy rains. She was low on supplies, as many of the injured natives had been making their way to her for help. She mixed Juan a potion by crushing some special roots and herbs, then combined them with a homemade brew poured from several recycled plastic Coca Cola bottles. She chanted as she concocted the medicine, sending prayers to the spirits to heal this child. She told the family that the medicine she gave him would also help the boy sleep and she would prepare tools for a ritual she would do on him that evening to draw out the fever.

Drew and Reagan heard of the little boy and his symptoms when they returned from their adventurous day and were both immediately concerned. They knew the clinic at Esperanza was recovering structurally from some flood damage and was temporarily closed until they could be sure everything was sanitized and safe, so using the diagnostic laboratory there would not be possible.

Mosquitos were always a problem in the rainforest, but the recent flooding and standing pools of water in the jungle, brought an onslaught of these pests and with certain types of mosquitos came grave illnesses, like malaria and dengue fever. Having traveled with physician groups to jungles in other parts of the world, the men were well aware of the symptoms which were similar in both diseases. They logically discussed the boy's situation.

"We know that dengue is caused by viruses transmitted by mosquitoes, producing flu-like symptoms—a high fever and maybe a severe headache; pain behind the eyes; joint, muscle, bone pain; rash; low white cell count; and in some cases, mild bleeding of the nose or gums, and easy bruising," Reagan logically noted.

Drew added, "We need to see this boy right away. As many as 400 million people are infected every year and there are no vaccines to prevent infection with the dengue virus. Thankfully, early recognition and treatment can lower the risk of medical complications and death. We can't take any chances."

The men walked to Rosita's hut, accompanied by Sydney and Dolly. When Juan awoke, the doctors examined him.

"I'm Doctor Drew and this is Doctor Reagan. Is it OK if we take a look at you?" Drew asked in Spanish, as he opened his doctor's bag and fetched a thermometer. The boy just stared at them weary-eyed and weak.

"How long have you been feeling sick? When did you start feeling feverish?" he asked. He knew that in dengue fever, the temperature declines three to seven days after symptoms begin. Time is not measured in days in the jungle, especially now, when each day of hard work ran into another as they labored to restore the village. The boy simply shrugged his shoulders. Pride would not have allowed him to complain of not feeling well when there was so much important work to be done, but he knew he had been feeling poorly for much too long.

"Have you had stomach pain or been vomiting?" Reagan asked as he noticed some red spots, a rash, on Juan's skin. "Have you had nose bleeds or trouble breathing?"

The boy shook his head, "No." That was a good sign. The doctors knew that advanced stages could mean dengue hemorrhagic fever where the smallest blood vessels become excessively leaky, allowing fluid to escape. This could lead to failure of the circulatory system and shock, and possibly death without prompt, appropriate treatment, which includes fluid replacement therapy. The clinic at Esperanza was not equipped for that.

After a thorough examination, the men reluctantly watched as Rosita took over again and administered another dose of her potion to the boy. Asking what was in the mixture only brought them irritation, as none of the jungle ingredients were familiar to them. The doctors stepped outside to confer.

Drew surmised, "We need to help this boy. We don't know if that concoction she is giving him will help before it's too late. He's really sick. This could be serious. With the clinic not yet back in use, we don't have any way of doing the lab work we need. Dengue fever is called 'break-bone fever' because of agonizing muscle and joint pain. All we can do here is offer Juan pain relievers. He needs plenty of fluids to prevent dehydration, and a lot of rest until we can transport him to Iquitos to a hospital."

"Yes, I agree, but his symptoms also parallel malaria—fever, chills and flu-like symptoms. If he has malaria, how we treat him depends on the species of the infecting mosquito, the boy's general health, allergies, and other medications," Reagan stated. "We don't know what's in the brew the shaman gave him and if that would affect any treatment we have. Left untreated, severe complications can develop, even death."

Sydney had followed the doctors outside and was listening to their technical diagnostic conversations. "The nurse at the clinic once told me that at one time they stocked chloroquine, quinine, and Lariam, but their supplies became outdated because malaria-carrying mosquitos don't breed in the Tahuayo River basin. This area doesn't have the ecosystem and the white sand forest habitat to support those species. So now they would rely on herbal brews to cure malaria if it should ever occur in the villages," she offered. "Rosita and Maria are used to dealing with these types of issues and know how to treat their patients. You should trust them. Maria has sent a canoe to a neighboring village for the herbs she'll need to help Rosita with the boy."

"She's wasting her time. We need to diagnose the illness before we can determine what the correct treatment is," replied Drew with an air of medical authority.

"We know there's only one species of mosquito in the tropical Americas that carries malaria, Anopheles darlingi, however, it does carry other species and subspecies of the malarial parasites. First, we have to find out what type of mosquitos breed in this area," he dismissed Sydney's information of malaria breeding mosquitos not being found in the region.

"Some species can cause rapidly progressive illness or death while the other species are less severe. Some infections require treatment for forms that remain dormant in the liver and can cause relapsing infections. Other species have different drug resistance patterns depending on geographic regions. The urgent use of appropriate therapy is especially critical, Sydney. Does your shaman know that?"

Sydney didn't like Drew's condescending attitude. He completely ignored what she had said about the local ecosystem not supporting malaria mosquito species, and she felt like he was pretty much accusing Rosita of being a quack. Sydney knew better from previous experiences.

Reagan added, "If it is malaria, even if we haven't confirmed that, antimalarial treatment must begin immediately."

"The river guides here are well versed in what mosquito species thrive in the area," Sydney said, forcefully. "Talk to them if you don't believe me. They've been here all their lives, are educated, and know more than what you give them credit for."

"This might be more than they can handle," Drew replied. "We know what we're doing, Sydney. Let us do our job."

Sydney understood where Drew was coming from, seeing his logic as a doctor, but he didn't know everything. He didn't know the power of a jungle shaman or the knowledge of the local guides. It irritated her that the two doctors seemed to dismiss the alternative healing of Rosita and Maria, assuming native training and methods were inferior to their own educated traditional treatments. Sydney had witnessed shaman and traditional healers around the world and knew how effective their medicine could be. She had to walk away from Drew and Reagan before she said things she might regret. She was angry. Both men had suddenly become foreign to her.

Sydney tried to cool her temper and went back into the hut to confer with Dolly about Rosita's evening healing ritual on Juan. Thinking it might humble them a little, she asked permission for the doctors to observe so they, too, could witness the magical blending of spiritual and alternative healing. Sydney had great faith in the old shaman's ability to heal the boy. . .but she was losing faith in the doctors.

twelve

THE SHAMAN'S BREATH

"You want us to sit in on your shaman's voodoo ceremony tonight?" Drew asked, almost mocking the situation. "Trust me, we're doing everything we can until we transport the boy to a hospital in Iquitos tomorrow. We're getting what supplies we can from the clinic in Esperanza and we'll both stay at his bedside through the night to monitor him. We'll take care of him."

Reagan nodded in agreement. "We took some blood samples, but will also need a sample of the brew your shaman gave him to have it analyzed to be sure it doesn't interfere with the medicine we'll have to prescribe."

This was a side of Drew and Reagan that Sydney hadn't expected. They were professionals, she realized that, but they weren't in the States. They were in the jungle. Everyone was grateful for all their expertise in the clinic, but now they were completely taking over in a situation that wasn't theirs to command. Juan's parents called on the shaman to heal their son. It was their culture. Their choice. They had confidence in Rosita. They trusted her with their son's life. They hadn't asked for the doctors' help.

"We've got it taken care of Sydney. That's why we're here. I'm sure we know more about medicine and can do more for the boy than the witchcraft of a village healer."

"Witchcraft! Aren't you being a bit arrogant?" she accused, feeling her anger rise. "Surely you must have encountered alternative healing during your doctor travels to the other jungles you spoke of? Did you discount their ability as voodoo, too? Have you no respect?"

"I'm sorry. That was a poor choice of words. I meant no disrespect. But why do you think we went to help in those places?" Drew responded, raising his voice in defense. "We were needed because local methods didn't work. We've studied years to be physicians. We aren't being arrogant. We are trained to help people. It's what we do. Why can't you understand that?"

"Of course I know that and your skills are appreciated," Sydney countered, realizing that Drew was clueless. He had kicked into his doctor mode and his mind worked along a single scientific path.

"But don't you think there may be other ways that work too? Where do you think your prescribed medicine comes from—these very jungles. The herbs and concoctions you so quickly dismiss have been used for hundreds of years before the big pharmaceutical companies got ahold of them and branded them. You need to trust that Rosita, Maria, and other medicine men and women like them know what they're doing, too. Their pharmacy is the jungle. Their nurses are the spirits of the plants and those on the other side who assist in the healing. These ways have been practiced for years in the jungle and it works. They may not have attended fancy, expensive medical schools, but this kind of healing has been handed down through generations. Their school is life."

"Life. . .and death," Drew somberly asserted. "We can't let this boy die. It's that critical, Sydney. I won't let this boy die."

"And you think Rosita will let him die?" The look on Sydney's face said it all. She was shocked at his disrespect for anything except what he had learned as a traditional doctor.

"You're so wrong. Don't be arrogant and insult the local healers with your ego-driven doctor-superiority attitude. If you feel that way you can just go back to your sterile hospital and big pharmaceutical-driven, prescription-writing practice. The village will survive without your medicine. It has before. It will continue to do so." Sydney's face was red with anger.

Drew and Reagan were surprised at her outburst. They didn't have words to respond. They were just doing what they were trained to do. Sydney began to walk away, then took a long breath to calm her emotions. She turned and slowly said, "I've arranged for you to sit in on Rosita's healing ceremony tonight with Juan. Swallow your pride and come if you like. . . or just stay away if you think you're so much better." She walked away before she completely lost control.

"Sydney. . ." Drew called after her, but she swiftly retreated. He knew better than to follow.

~~~~~

Sydney, Dolly, a few other lodge staff, along with Juan's family, sat in a semi-circle around Rosita on the wooden floor of her thatched hut. Their purpose was to hold positive energy for the healing that was to take place. Sydney had permission from Rosita to photograph during the healing, so, always documenting, she set up her camera on a small tripod, trying to be as discrete as possible. She didn't want it to interfere with any of the ceremony.

In the center, lying on a pile of blankets was Juan, still shaking, almost convulsing, hot and cold with fever. Sydney saw Reagan arrive and take a seat opposite the door, but she did not see Drew. It saddened and infuriated her that he would be so dismissive of the shaman's ability to not even attend the healing. Wasn't he at least curious?

"I knew this relationship was too good to be true," she reprimanded herself for falling so fast, so hard. She hadn't anticipated this "superior" side of Drew and now her emotions were becoming mixed about their affair. She would have been better off keeping to her "one year" rule. It would have made her life so much easier. She forced herself to put thoughts of Drew aside as the healing ceremony began.

Rosita was in her late 80s and had been trained as a healer since she was 14 by her uncle in the high Andes. She was Chino Village's midwife and shaman. The old woman began her ritual by lighting a candle in the center of the circle. Her "tools" were nearby—a large half gourd bowl; another gourd with water; branches of dried shapaca (sha-pa-ca) leaves that were tied into a small bundle to make a shaking rattle to call on the spirits; a knife to shave curls of bark off a branch of ajo-sacha (ah-ho-sa-cha), or wild false garlic; chuchuhuasi (chu-chu-wasi), a mixture made from four barks: pure chuchuhuasi, turtle sandango, sugar cane rum with honey, and ajo-sacha juice. This and other brews were contained in plastic liter Coca Cola and 7-Up bottles. A pile of fresh tobacco was spread out on a newspaper, its pungent nicotine-rich leaves spewing out onto the wooden floorboards, dropping through the cracks to the rain-washed, muddy ground below.

When Rosita finished whittling the false garlic root, she placed the shavings into the gourd bowl and added sugar cane rum to it from one of the plastic bottles. Using her hand to mix it, she let it soak to absorb the garlic's medicine. When this mixture was ready, she handed the bowl to Sydney on her right. Sydney took a sip and passed the bowl on. It went around the room and everyone drank the strong juice. Dolly and Juan's mother helped the boy drink from a smaller bowl that had been filled from the large gourd. The gourd was passed around twice and Sydney was glad to noticed that Reagan participated in the ceremony. She couldn't help but wish that Drew was there to experience the ritual. Why must he be so stubborn? This was not voodoo, as he so harshly accused. It was ancient native medicine—pure nature/spirit communion with one goal, to heal the patient.

Rosita picked up the bundle of shapaca leaves and began to shake them over Juan, softly singing hauntingly beautiful songs, one of which was "the garlic song," calling plant spirits to help heal this boy. After this, she rolled sacred tobacco into a cigarette, lit it and taking long drags, she blew smoke over Juan's body, chanting more songs in-between inhales. She continued to shake the shapaca leaves, blowing smoke and singing for nearly half an hour, sometimes looking up into the air, receiving messages from the spirits as to the root of Juan's illness and what she should do to help him.

Rosita was in her own world of visions, a conduit for healing. After blowing the smoke of several cigarettes around the body and taking more sips from the potent gourd liquid, Rosita began to swirl her hands over the boy's body, as if the spirits had diagnosed the affliction and now she was centering in on the illness. She'd stop in certain areas where she felt heat and, without actually touching the boy, would make motions as if she were pulling something out of him—long strands of illness, sick energy, fever, darkness or evil spells, whatever was contaminating the boy. She gathered invisible gobs of bad substance from the body and placed them into the gourd of water. This went on for several minutes. Then she positioned herself at the head of the boy and forming a cone with her hands, she blew into the top of his head.

Sydney had witnessed this many times before with Rosita and healers in other parts of the world, and she knew that Rosita was sending the boy's power animal into his body to help heal from the inside—to strengthen him and bring him through his healing journey. This was followed by more hand motion, smoothing out the body, more rattle shaking and chanting. The bowl of water with the impure energy was brought outside by Maria and respectfully dumped at the base of a tree with a prayer that this residue would dissipate back into the air and turn into positive energy.

When Rosita was finished, she sat back and nodded her head toward Juan's parents, an affirmation that the healing was complete. She confidently said that when Juan, who was now sound asleep and breathing peacefully, awoke in the morning, his fever would be gone and he would be back to normal. He would be cured. She told his mother to let him sleep there for the night and welcomed them to sleep in her house near him also. She said his power animal, a puma, would guard over him now, help restore his strength and keep him safe.

Sydney packed up her camera equipment and left with the staff, reverently walking into the dark silence of the star-studded night to boats waiting to transport them back to the lodge. A pink dolphin jumped in the black water near the shore. The sound of an animal called out from the thick jungle walls —the echoing roar of a puma. No one spoke a word.

~~~~~

Sydney lingered in the dining hall when she returned to the lodge, talking with Dolly for awhile about Rosita, Juan and the evening events. She confided her thoughts about Drew, about her disappointment in his disrespect for Rosita and her abilities.

Dolly told Sydney that she was being too harsh. "We see that often here," she sadly admitted. "But sometimes, after the doctors and nurses come and see what miraculous things our herbalists and local shaman are doing, they often become the students. They realize there's room to explore other elements in the world of healing, and that we can all learn from each other. It's not mystical talk and sorcery. It's real medicine. You and I know that. I'm sure your doctor friends will come to realize it too."

"Thank you. You're so wise," Sydney said, giving Dolly a genuine hug. "I needed to hear that. I guess I really did overreact defending Rosita and the other healers here. I just respect them and their work so much."

When Dolly left, Sydney stayed in the dining hall to write in her journal. She had a lot of emotions to work though.

Reagan startled her when he sat down beside her.

"How long have you been here?" she asked.

"Not long," he said, looking around. "I couldn't sleep."

"That was quite impressive—the ritual tonight," he admitted. "But, do you really believe what she did will heal the boy?"

"Absolutely," Sydney answered without delay. "I believe in the power and the mystery of the spirits that magically work through Rosita."

Reagan was silent.

"I came down pretty hard on you and Drew tonight. I'm sorry," Sydney was taking Dolly's advice.

"Apology accepted. But you were right in some of what you said. Sometimes I think we've been brainwashed to think our way is the only way. I can see there is more to it. I do want to know more about this shaman woman, Rosita. What can you tell me about her?"

"Several years ago she told me that she was married to a shaman in the village. She made the medicine for him from medicinal herbs, potions she had learned as a young girl. Another village shaman was jealous. He was lazy and wanted her for his wife, so she could make his medicine instead. He put a spell on her husband and drowned him in the river. Then he used witchcraft on Rosita and she married him. He used a lot of ayahuasca and eventually became incapacitated. I remember meeting him many years ago and he just laid in a corner on the tambo in a stupor. He was pretty burned out. I don't know when he died. Rosita said that sometimes now when she needs help to find a remedy, she goes to the river where her first husband drowned and he appears to her in the form of a pink river dolphin. She connects with his spirit and he gives her the answers she needs."

"A dolphin!" Reagan exclaimed! "Did you see the dolphin splash by our boat when we left?"

Sydney just smiled.

"Amazing. And did you hear that cat roaring in the jungle when we got into the boat? The shaman said Juan's healing animal was a puma! It was eerie." Reagan shook his head. "You really believe her medicine and ritual will pull the boy through, don't you?"

"Yes I do. You don't realize that she has an entire team of spirits working through her. Rosita says this gift was given to her to help people. And she does, every day of her life. Selflessly, honorably and in deep gratitude to those spirits who believe in her. There's great magic here in the jungle."

Reagan stared at Sydney for a few moments. "You shouldn't be so hard on him, you know," he finally said.

"Who?"

"You know who I mean. Drew. And he'll probably be angry for me telling you this, but he *was* there tonight, in the shadows, so you couldn't see him."

"That makes me even angrier," Sydney quickly replied. "That he didn't have enough guts to admit he might be wrong and show himself. I guess I don't know him as well as I thought."

"He took to heart what you said about being close minded and was pretty offended. He has a stubborn streak, but it goes deeper than that. You don't know what he's been through, Sydney."

She looked at Reagan. "Why did you come to the ceremony tonight?"

"I was curious. I had nothing to lose. I'm glad I participated." Reagan hesitated, listening to the sound of the lodge's motor boat dwindled into a distant buzz as it made its way down river with only flashlights to guide its way.

"What is it?" Sydney caught his expression.

"I don't know how much Drew told you about his marriage and it's probably not my place to say. . .but. . . his wife was pregnant when she died. He not only lost his wife, but also a child. A son. You must understand that for him to see that young boy so ill and watch a shaman work unfamiliar mystical wonders that are suppose to suddenly cure him, well, that goes against everything he's learned in his practice as a doctor. He's clinical, practical. . .he's a doctor, a man of science. It's hard for him to leave anything to chance. He would blame himself if this boy died and he didn't help him."

"That's absurd," Sydney said. "It wouldn't be his fault."

"I'm just telling you. That's the way Drew thinks. He's completely dedicated to his practice—like Rosita is to hers."

Sydney thought for a moment. "Should I go talk with him? Do you think it would help? I said some pretty terrible things."

"It's a little late for that," Reagan replied. "He knows you're angry. He thinks he blew it with you, that you've completely lost respect for him. And, let's face it, he's a bit insulted. He just left in that boat you heard, for Iquitos. He thinks Juan has malaria. If the parents won't let Juan be transported to the hospital, Drew thought he could at least bring the blood samples in to be diagnosed to see if he can get medicine to help the boy. He's that dedicated."

"But it takes four hours in the daylight to get to Iquitos. It's very dangerous at night. Couldn't he have waited until morning to at least see how Juan was feeling?"

"Drew didn't want to waste any time and he can be very convincing. Arturo is a good boatman and Augusto went along to watch for logs and obstacles in the river. They were going to bring other supplies back for the villagers too, so it will be a productive trip all around. Don't worry about them. Augusto assured me they'd be fine. They'll be back in two days and hopefully will have medicine for Juan and at least know his diagnosis.

"There's something else you might like to know about Drew to help you understand how dedicated he is to his profession," Reagan began. "Part of the reason we're here is because Drew is on leave from the hospital. . . because, well, there was a problem and Drew was asked to take a break. I just came along because he's my friend and I support him in any way I can. He's a good man."

"What happened?" Sydney was curious.

"It's an issue of not following hospital protocol. Short story, an elderly man needed emergency treatment and had no insurance. The hospital's policy forced them to turned him away. Drew went behind the hospital's back and found a way to provide the treatment, which probably saved the man's life. The board was furious and Drew was reprimanded for bending the rules, treating the man without proper paperwork, what if they got sued, etc., etc. Right now he's on suspension, pending review. The hospital added extra stress to the old man by demanding immediate full payment for the treatment. Drew quietly paid the man's bill out of his own pocket. I'm the only other person who knows this. The man he helped doesn't even know who paid the bill. So when you accused Drew of being disrespectful and arrogant, it probably struck a nerve. He's really pretty awesome."

Sydney was so touched, she felt tears swelling in her eyes. "Now I really feel like a fool," she shamefully admitted. "I should have had more faith in his character than to accuse him of anything. I overreacted. He must think I'm a real bitch and won't ever want to see me again."

"The important thing now is to check on Juan in the morning to see how he's doing. Drew wanted me to stay with him during the night, but his parents insisted they can take care of him with Rosita there. I hope they're right. I wouldn't mind witnessing a medical miracle."

"Call it what you want—miracle, magic, voodoo. Rosita is a powerful shaman and I have no doubt that Juan will be up and ready to go in a few days. You'll see."

With that, she gave Reagan a goodnight pat on the shoulder and headed off down the creaky wooden walkway to her room, alone with her thoughts and her longing for Drew, the man she may have just driven out of her life forever.

~ thirteen ~

REVELATIONS

Sydney was miserable. She was having deep remorse for the things she said to Drew, especially after what Reagan had shared with her about Drew not only losing his wife, but also his unborn son. She understood now why he had been so driven to help Juan.

"How could I have been so judgmental? It appears that I'm the one who was disrespectful," she admonished herself.

Drew may have been stubborn and focused on his own methods, but she was the one who had really screwed up this time. Everything had been so perfect between them. They may have different perspectives when it comes to medicine, but she could have handled it better and not gotten so angry. She couldn't expect to just apologize and think that things would go back the way they were. He was hurt by her accusations of him being egocentric. How could he respect her now? It was futile. She couldn't face him. She didn't deserve him.

The insecurities of past failed romances flooded back to her. She needed to get away. She needed to bury herself deeper into the jungle. Drew would be better without her.

The next day Sydney made arrangements to transfer to ARC, Amazonia Research Center, Tahuayo River Lodge's other facility, about an hour up river. It was in remote, pristine forest with the largest trail grid system in the Amazon, covering 52 miles spread over 1,000 acres. Even though it was world renown and connected with prestigious research centers, like Yale University, only a couple of scientist were presently in residence, plus the site manager. It would be a good place to hide away and sulk in her misery. Sydney asked Reagan and Dolly to simply tell Drew that she had left, if he asked about her. It wasn't a lie. She had left the main lodge. Sydney wondered if he would even bother to ask. He had seen a side of her that he most likely didn't want to see again.

But first she had to see about Juan and his progress. It didn't surprise Sydney at all when a canoe glided up to the dock as Ricardo was preparing for Sydney and Reagan to go to the village. Juan's father expertly guided his dugout canoe next to the landing and Juan greeted them with a big grin. As Rosita promised, the boy was completely healed. No fever, no rash. He was back to his energetic self.

"I don't believe it," Reagan managed. "Is this the same boy from last night?"

Reagan asked if it was all right if he examined Juan, just to compare his vitals to his last exam. Juan's father nodded in agreement, as if to boast, "We'll show you how good our jungle medicine is. Here's your proof."

"I may as well grab my backpack and camera bag and head to the research center," Sydney said to Ricardo. She ruffled Juan's thick black hair. "I knew I'd see your bright smile again. I'm happy you're well." A few minutes later she was on her way to her remote retreat.

~~~~~

Drew was feeling depressed. Not only had he had little sleep while on his personal quest to save Juan, but he couldn't stop thinking about Sydney.

"Maybe she was right," he thought. Maybe his ego about being an educated doctor and having to do things his way had driven him to act superior. He was sorry he hadn't been more open minded and at least acknowledged the shaman's skills. He also realized that he loved Sydney. It was a big step for him to open up his heart again. He didn't want to lose her.

Reagan greeted Drew in the dining hall when he heard of his return.

"I was wrong about the malaria. Juan's blood results says he has dengue fever," Drew reported, looking fatigued.

"It doesn't matter," Reagan said, then excitedly told him about Juan's complete recovery, going over his most recent medical stats. Drew was dumbfounded.

". . .are you sure. . .it's hard to believe these results are from the same boy. And you examined him completely? He's clear of all symptoms?"

Drew and Reagan discussed Juan at length, dissecting what had transpired during Rosita's healing ritual. None of it made any sense to Drew, but whatever she had done, it seemed to have worked.

"I guess I owe an apology to Juan's 'physician,' Rosita, for doubting her medicine," Drew concluded. "And to Sydney. Have you seen her around?"

Reagan hesitated. "She's not here. I mean, she left."

"Left! Where did she go?"

"She left yesterday, Drew. I'm sorry man. She didn't think you'd want to see her again after the things she said to you and thought she'd make it easier for both of you." This was true. Reagan didn't want to lie to his best friend, but he was put into a tough position.

Drew was silent. She was gone.

Reagan tried to change the subject. "We still have work to do here, Doctor. We promised a couple more days at the clinic. They are up and running again, including the diagnostic lab, so maybe you can do some comparisons with the blood samples I took from Juan yesterday with the results from Iquitos. I'd also like to make another round in

Chino Village to follow up on flood injuries. I thought you'd want to join me."

Drew still didn't speak. He was processing.

"I'd like to see if Dolly can arrange for me to meet with Rosita and Maria. It seems there's a lot we can learn from them," he slowly admitted, knowing his last week in the jungle wouldn't be the same without Sydney. He could at least be productive. Maybe it would take his mind off her, although he doubted it. Just the thought of her filled his senses—the smell of her hair, the softness of her skin, her sweet, tantalizing smile and sense of humor . . .their lovemaking. . .their wild uninhibited lovemaking. . . Truth is, Drew didn't want to get those images out of his mind. He just wanted Sydney back in his arms.

~~~~~

After two days assisting at the clinic, the men headed to Chino with Augusto as translator to visit Rosita. She was seated on the floor of her hut, with a backstrap loom around her waist, weaving a long, white piece of cloth. She had spun the cotton herself, using fibers gathered from pods of the kapok tree, using a crude wooden spindle that was laying in a basket of round balls of her handmade threads. Nearby was also a handmade potter's wheel she used to make her own dishes out of river mud. This was an amazing woman.

Rosita graciously acknowledged the doctors and they sat with her for the entire day, listening to stories of how she works with her spirit guides and about what plants she used in her medicines. She told them how she prepared poultices and tinctures from jungle plants. She also sent for Maria who had been been busy trying to locate more medicinal plants, her "pharmaceutical" supplies, from the jungle to transplant into a new garden, along with the plants Augusto and Ricardo had dug for her earlier. Rosita and Maria often worked together in their role as healers. There could never be too many curanderos, healers, in a jungle village.

The men learned about the spirit of the plants and how they speak to the women to show them how to diagnose and to heal. They explained how each plant has a signature sign on it that corresponds with the illness. Red blooms or red leaves were used for blood problems, as in parts of the rose plant being used for stopping excess bleeding. The doctors would never look at another plant with the same eyes again.

"If you come in contact with a plant that, let's say, gives you a scratchy rash," Maria explained, "there will always be the antidote plant growing nearby. You just have to know what to look for. Before you leave we can do a jungle herb walk and I can show you some of the plants we harvest and explain what they can do."

"When we go back to Iquitos I'll take you to Belen," Augusto offered. "There's a huge street market where all of these roots and plants are sold. Most of your medicine originally came from these types of plants. At least those that are not commercially grown and modified," he added.

"You must also go to our research center. There are two scientists from Switzerland there now who are studying medicinal plants that grow near the grid we've marked out for research. You'll find their discoveries very interesting."

"I'd like that," Drew responded. "All of it. Let's make arrangements as soon as possible." This was like going back to college and he was suddenly excited about all the possibilities this jungle had to offer. If only he had made this observation earlier in his stay, things would have been different between him and Sydney.

Reagan winced when Augusto suggested the research center visit, but he decided that things will play out as they should and he certainly didn't want to get any more involved than he already was. He, for one, thought Drew and Sydney made a perfect couple.

But before Drew could go anywhere, Dolly approached him and invited him to sit with her in the dining hall. She had something to show him.

"I hope this isn't inappropriate, Drew, but Sydney is a good friend of mine and she's spoken to me about your. . .friendship. I wanted you to get a sense of why she's so passionate about the mysterious ways of the jungle. This is a copy of an entry from one of her journals. She shared it with me the first time she came here. I don't think she'd mind if you read it."

Dolly handed a copy of the handwritten journal entry to Drew. It was several pages long.

— THE DREAM..."A sense of peaceful adventure surrounded me as I entered the untamed world of Amazonia. Walking down a vine entangled path I

came upon a small clearing. A filtered patch of sunlight beamed through the cashapona trees onto the leafy jungle floor. I stopped to breathe in the splendor of this paradise and listen to the melodious song of hundreds of birds and the constant chatter of monkeys. It was hot, yet sunlight through a window in the thick jungle canopy was inviting.

Suddenly, the jungle stilled. Crickets stopped screeching, birds silenced their song and monkeys seemed motionless in the trees. I felt a sharp pain as I was struck from behind. Everything fell into slow motion. Instead of a clean strike the anaconda was clinging to my leg. Its jaws spread open around my bleeding flesh, clamped like a vise without means or desire to release its grip. I fell to the ground, the musty smells of the forest floor permeated my nostrils and I lost consciousness.

In an instant my spirit floated upward and I viewed the scene from a few feet above my body. My khaki-clothed form lay within the moist flora of the rainforest floor. Nearby, leaf-cutter ants formed an unbroken line, carrying portions of leaves to their homes. They paid no attention to the fallen giant near their path. The snake, too, lay silent, jaws locked, eyes glaring in a trancelike state. My *unconscious mind calmly took control and commanded the snake to release its grip and leave. It was not a roaring command. It was an unspoken voice of authority. Of power. The anaconda, eyes still glazed, released its mighty grip and slowly slithered into the green wall of jungle, as if obeying a superior being.*

My spirit hovered over my body for a time sending healing energy into the wounded leg. Spirit passed a hand of light over the leg and the wound disappeared. Then Spirit reentered my body. I became conscious, sat up and watched the last link of slithering snake disappear into the bushes. Without any fear or questioning of what had just happened, I arose and continued on my way, as if I just experienced a common occurrence."—

"Wow," Drew exclaimed. "That's powerful."

"Yes, it is," Dolly said. "This was a dream Sydney had before she came to the jungle the very first time, many years ago. She met with a favorite shaman of ours, Cumpanam. They had quite a connection. Read on."

—The Achuara shaman, Cumpanam, looked at me. His intense black eyes fixed on mine as I finished telling him about my dream. His tanned, weathered face was serious as he pondered what I had just told him. He spoke Achuara and Spanish. I spoke only English. My jungle guide, Jose, interpreted.

"When did you have this dream?" the shaman asked.

"Three nights before coming to the Amazon," I responded.

"Were you afraid?"

I said "No."

He questioned me further. "Are you afraid now that you are here?"

Again my answer was "No."

He nodded, said "Good," then lowered his head and continued carving shavings from an ajo-sacha, false garlic, vine.

Silence. I kept looking at Jose for a sign of what to do. I had walked a mile through the jungle to the shaman's village, Jerusalem, to hear this answer? Jose sat quietly, watching the shaman shave medicine from the vine into a gourd bowl. Sensing my impatience, Jose filled in the silence, explaining that the shaman was making an important medicine mixture for a healing he would do in our camp tonight for a man with asthma. The shaman said prayers while he worked with the plants. More silence. Finally he spoke.

"Have you had other dreams like this?"

"No, but I did have a dream that I was supposed to look for some sort of medicine stick on this trip. Was the snake my medicine stick?" I asked.

"No," he answered. He went back to his shavings.

Silence. I waited. Finally the shaman rose, dusted off his trousers and said, "When I come to your camp tonight I will make a ceremony for you. We will find out about this medicine stick and your dreams." Then he walked away.

That night. . .I could hear him in the distance, singing and chanting as he worked, healing the asthmatic man. I sat on my sleeping bag, inside my mosquito net enclosure, writing in my journal, anxiously awaiting my turn. The blackness of the night engulfed the tambo, which was raised on stilts above the ground to accommodate the wet season of the Amazon. Candles and kerosene lanterns dimly lit the camp. Finally, I heard the creak of crude floorboards as the shaman and Jose followed the walkway leading toward me. Their shadows loomed *like dinosaurs on the loose weave of my mosquito netting. We cordially nodded toward each other and then sat in a triangle around a single candle.*

The shaman chanted and sang in low whispers, whistled through his teeth and made motions with his hands. He rolled black tobacco into a leaf and blew smoke all around me. He handed me a smooth amber colored stone, his healing stone, telling me to rub it on my body and hold it in my hand. It would absorb my energy. Then he read the stone.

This medicine man sprinkled garlic ajo-sacha into his gourd bowl, tossed in a handful of black tobacco, mashed in sugar cane root and manioc, and mixed it all together with other roots and herbs. To this he added river water and then handed it to me to drink. I reluctantly took a sip and nearly gagged. It was bad. He continued his smoke blowing and chanting and every once in a while stopped and handed me the gourd to take another drink. He kept asking me if I was dizzy or had to throw up. Although the potion tasted terrible, I wasn't nauseated.

The ceremony continued and I wondered if his goal was to make me keep drinking until I was sick.

I prayed he wouldn't make me finish drinking the entire thing.

"Am I supposed to vomit?" I finally asked.

"Vomiting gets rid of dark and evil spirits and poisons in the body," he explained. He was pleased that I didn't have to vomit. It meant that I was free of illness and dark spirits. It was good.

The ceremony lasted an hour and a half and ended with a healing ritual, summoning the Spirits to protect me. He told them that I was also a shaman and asked these Spirits to stay with me through my earthly journey. This was news to me. The shaman also told me that in a few nights I would dream again and he would interpret that dream to give me the answers I was looking for.

He added "If anyone tries to give you a gift, you should accept it. No matter what it is. Accept it. It is important." I nodded. He turned and walked quietly into the deep darkness of the jungle night.

The taste of black tobacco stained my mouth and throat and I couldn't swallow it away. I didn't dream that night.—

Drew paused. "He told Sydney she was a shaman? What did he mean by that? Is she a healer too?"

Dolly instructed him to continue reading. "Enjoy her adventure."

—*Later, we were on a three day jungle survival trip, up a small tributary of the Blanquillo River. Cumpanam and guides, Ashuco and Jose, had literally chopped our way through trees and vines that appeared as the river level dropped.*

It had taken us nearly two days to travel what normally took three hours. Along the way the shaman called to birds in the thick rainforest and they answered his call. He shouted to the monkeys and after a short time we heard crashing noises through the trees. An entire clan of rare Uakari monkeys responded and came with curiosity to see us. They hung around, swinging overhead, answering the hoots and grunts of the shaman. Then they noisily returned the way they had come.

The men pointed out jaguar, ocelot, tapir and anteater tracks along the river bank. Ashuco, our boatman pointed to a small inlet and we paddled toward the bank for a better look. Coiled among the fresh, flowing water was a huge anaconda. The snake was at least twelve inches around with eyes the size of quarters. It was soothing itself with a massage of swift water flowing into the river. The shaman got out of the boat and edged toward the anaconda. The snake didn't move.

The shaman looked at me.

"Is this the anaconda in your dream?" he asked.

"This one is much larger," I replied.

"Are you afraid?"

I was surprised at my calm. All I could think about was how beautiful it was, all shiny and glistening with the sunlight playing on the water over its back.

"No," I answered.

He reached for a stick and poked the snake gently. It uncoiled, and slowly slithered into the river, right next to our boat. An electric eel flashed as the snake swam by. The snake was over 16 feet long. Achuco estimated it weighed 80 to 100 pounds and noted that it had survived to grow so big because we were in a little traveled area of the jungle. Natives rarely come here.

As darkness invaded we sparingly used flashlights to find our way up river. My senses were filled with the sounds and smells of jungle. Hundreds of species of tree frogs chorused, roared and sang throughout the night. At one point the shaman directed me to shine my light into the water. His keen eye concentrated for several minutes and suddenly he reached into the depths and snatched out a two foot long long baby caiman from the splashing water. The caiman's eyes reflected with surprise in the light of my flashlight as it wriggled and wrenched to free itself.

"Cumpashin!" the shaman proudly yelled, "Cumpashin!" which roughly translates as "I am a good friend."

He held it tightly so I could touch its leathery skin and then gently released it back into the water.

We finally set up a makeshift camp, clearing an area with machetes to hang our mosquito netting. Recalling the anaconda, caiman and animal tracks we had seen, I knew I wouldn't sleep well. This was raw, virgin jungle and it was an adventure to be here, yet I was mindful of the dangers. I was sleeping in the wild Amazon jungle in a very remote area, with only thin mosquito netting between me and predatory animals. Just taking a few steps into the dark jungle to go to the bathroom could be disastrous. I hoped the Spirits Cumpanam asked to guide me would protect me through the tonight.

The thick canopy of trees hid any trace of stars or moonlight. It was pitch black. I tucked my netting in tightly under the thin mattress which was padded by palm fronds, hoping to keep snakes, bugs or animals from invading my space. It was a restless night, yet a chorus of tree frogs and crickets blending with sounds of the flowing river was an inviting symphony that eventually lulled me to sleep.

The following day the guides used their machetes to clear an overgrowth of brush and trees, chopping our way up river, finally reaching the Kapok tree which marked the spot of our entry into the jungle. We hiked for a strenuous three hours up and down mounds, around gigantic trees, through swamp and mud, rushing to reach our night camp before dark.

"We must be there before dark," Ashuco urged. "Snakes come out onto the trails at night and it could be dangerous." The very thought kept my adrenaline flowing and my feet moving. I was glad I hadn't known that the night before.

We reached a tambo, an open platform with a thatched roof, and stopped for a short rest. I sat on the rough bamboo flooring in the dense forest *writing in my journal. Suddenly I heard the loud buzzing of bees ascending upon us. The drone grew louder and louder. I looked up from my pages to see a thick cloud of large black bees flying all around me. I glanced over at the Cumpanam.*

A voice in my head said, "Don't be afraid. They can sense your fear. Be very still and they won't hurt you." Cumpanam was sitting and calmly watching me.

I closed my mouth tightly and took in long slow breaths through my nose, trying to squeeze my nostrils together as much as I could. I squinted so bees wouldn't get into my eyes, behind my sunglasses. My sweat bandana covered my ears and I was grateful to be wearing a long sleeved shirt, long pants, sox and boots. My shirt sleeves were rolled up to my elbows. I realized that I was the only person being swarmed by the insects. I could see my arms nearly covered with bees. They crawled, moving their feelers to test my skin. It tickled. I sat still and couldn't believe my calm. I was literally covered by hundreds of bees, perhaps, thousands, and I was not getting stung. Just as incredible, I was actually calmly sitting and observing the swarm! I totally trusted Cumpanam's confident assurance, the message in my head that told me that if I did not show fear I would not be harmed.

I actually began to feel like I was a part of the swarm. I was one of them. I was at their core. They were landing and flying all around me, yet I was strangely peaceful. I was accepted by them as simply another part of nature. I felt like I was the queen bee gathering her swarm around her for a reunion. I lost all track of time.

Gradually the bees started to leave. First a few flew away and then, as though a whistle had been blown, the rest flew off in unison. I watched the dark shadow of the swarm move through the trees. The music of their buzz distanced into the jungle. I wanted to shout after them and thank them—for what I'm not sure, but somehow I felt this experience was a gift of nature. Sitting still until the last straggler took flight, I looked at Cumpanam. He was nodding and smiling. I felt him beam a message to me that I had just passed some huge test of the jungle, a mystical shamanic initiation. —

"This is really intense!" Drew said as he looked up from the pages. "Did this really happen? How can she not acknowledge this gift and act like an everyday normal person?"

"Oh, now you're saying it's a gift, not voodoo?" Dolly challenged.

"Touché," Drew sheepishly replied.

"There's more. . ."

— *Sitting around the campfire that night, I listened to the shaman. He told of when he first began his shamanic journey. He stared into the fire as he described a dream he had when a beautiful woman appeared and said she would take care of him.*

"She represents the Spirit of the plants and she guides me in knowing how to prepare for healing," *he revealed. "The chanting during my ceremonies are prayers of thanks and requests for additional guidance." He added, "we must always remember to thank the plants and the Spirits."*

We sat silently, watching the flames of the fire dance into the night.

"I had a dream last night," I announced.

He didn't answer, just looked at me, waiting for me to continue. The black pupils of his eyes seemed to catch light from the campfire as they directed their gaze toward me.

"I was in a dugout canoe on the river. The water was smooth and clear, yet the river was very foggy. Suddenly another dugout canoe appeared out of the mist. In it was a sparsely dressed native man with long dark hair and a serious look on his face. He paddled up to my canoe, reached down and handed me a beautiful Bird-of-Paradise flower. I remembered what you said, and slowly reached out to accept the plant. He smiled and paddled away, disappearing into the fog."

The shaman stared at me for what seemed to be forever, shadows of the campfire playing on his thin brown face. I returned his gaze. Finally he spoke.

"You accepted the gift?"

"Yes."

"Good," he replied. "It is a good dream. The flower is your medicine stick. You must use it."

Silence.

"But what does it mean?" I asked. "How do I use it?"

Silence.

"You will understand the meaning of your dream when you are ready to accept the answer," he said firmly. "When you are ready to accept your destiny."

"What destiny?" I asked.

He reached over and retrieved his gourd of yuca or manioc mixture, taking a long drink. Then he motioned it toward me.

"What's in it?" I asked, wondering if it was the same awful concoction he had used during my healing ceremony.

"It is what I drink to summon the Spirits into my head to ask for answers in my healing." He pushed the gourd into my hands. "Drink," he said.

I looked at Jose. He nodded his head.

"It's an honor," Jose whispered. "I've never seen him offer his special potion to anyone before. Drink."

I accepted the gourd and took a drink of the sour mystical formula. The taste of terrible black tobacco burned down my throat. I tried not to make a face, to be brave. I smiled and handed the gourd back, offering a weak "Thank you."

When the shaman finished the drink he handed me his empty gourd bowl.

"Keep this," he said. "It is for you to use when you accept your role as a shaman."

He grabbed a branch and began to stir the campfire. Wild red flames snapped, reaching high

*into the Amazon sky. He watched them swirling
upward, burning themselves out. Their embers
disappearing into blackness.*

The shaman turned to me and smiled slightly.

"It is a good dream. A good dream," he repeated.

Drew looked up at Dolly in disbelief.

"So, Sydney is a shaman? No wonder she reacted
the way she did when I discounted Rosita's
medicine. Why didn't she tell me?"

"She didn't tell you because she hasn't really
accepted that part of herself yet. Her destiny. She
doesn't use plant medicine like Rosita and Maria,
but she knows she has the ability to heal, to call on
the spirits to work through her when she needs
them. She still has Cumpanam's medicine gourd. I
think that's why she comes back to the jungle over
and over again. She talks about balance, finding
something that's missing her life. She thinks it's
love. I think she longs to reclaim that part of her
that Cumpanam revealed. Rosita has told her the
same thing. She has powerful medicine, that
woman. She knows the Spirits are there when she's
ready. She just hasn't figured out how to use it yet,

or taken the time to work with the energy. She will. Someday."

"Thank you for sharing this with me, Dolly," Drew said as he handed back the journal notes. "You're right. It does help me to understand her better. It's almost a little frightening."

"It shouldn't be. If you see her again, don't treat her any differently because you know this. She's the same woman you've befriended. I'm just telling you that there is a lot more depth to Sydney Knight than you may realize. Respect that. Maybe someday, she'll finally come into her own shamanic power. She'll find out how to use that medicine stick."

Drew thanked Dolly again and walked slowly to his room. She had said *if* he ever saw Sydney again. He didn't like the sound of that. He had a lot to digest.

fourteen

RESOLUTIONS

Believing that Sydney had returned to New York, and not knowing if he would see her again, Drew did what he did best. He threw himself into his work. After reading the portion of Sydney's journal, he had a new respect for her beliefs. He spent his extra time taking jungle "pharmacy" walks with Maria and Rosita and devoured the lodge's library of local medicinal plants and legends of jungle spirits. He wondered why he hadn't noticed these shelves of books before. Reagan was just as interested. The two doctors had much to learn.

"I'm bringing supplies to the research center this afternoon," Augusto approached him one day. "We can arrange for you to stay there a couple of days to talk with the scientists who are studying our plants."

"Yes," Drew quickly accepted. "I've arranged to stay a few days longer and would like to do that before I head back home." He turned to Reagan. "Are you up for it, Doctor?"

Not wanting to get caught in a web of deception, Reagan excused himself, saying he just wanted to swing in a hammock, listen to the sounds of the jungle, eat and sleep for the last days of his trip. Maybe he'd do some more canopy zip lining and fishing. They had been very busy and he needed a real vacation.

Drew packed a few belongings and headed up river with Augusto, expecting nothing more than to quench his thirst for more knowledge. He arrived in the dim light of lanterns lining the boardwalk. Anxious to visit with the Swiss scientists about their work, he had just enough time to settle into his room before the deep beat of the drum announced that dinner was served.

~~~~~

Sydney didn't know why she had such an uneasy feeling as the day wore on. She had taken her retreat time at the research center seriously and made time to read, write in her journal, photograph, meditate, and relax. She was getting over her sulking and resolved herself to the fact that Drew truly was finished with her. He couldn't forgive her for their indifferences and the things she said to him. Her beliefs were rooted in the spirit world. His in the world of science. That was quite a leap to overcome.

Even though Sydney had asked Reagan and Dolly not to tell him where she was, deep down she wanted him to know. She wanted him to come to her and take her in his arms as if nothing had happened. Her mouth couldn't forget the taste of his love. Her dreams were filled with the ecstasy of their lovemaking and the security she felt next to him in bed afterward. It felt good. It had been almost a week and she hadn't heard a word from him. Her conclusion was that he had gone his own way without another thought of her. It was a fling that ended badly. It was over. Sadly over. She didn't regret that she had given herself to him so freely. She only regretted her misjudgment of his character and her unforgiving reaction to his stubbornness.

But tonight she felt anxious. Edgy. She understood why when she walked into the dining room. At first she thought she must have been mistaken. But as soon as he saw her, he jumped up and came over to greet her with a big hug. Shocked, she tried to push him away. She couldn't believe her eyes. It was Richard, the man she had come to the jungle to get away from. The man she no longer wanted in her life and certainly didn't want him here, in her jungle sanctuary.

"What? What the hell are you doing here?" she demanded.

"What kind of a greeting is that, after I've come all this way and spent all this money to see you?" he replied, trying to make her feel ungrateful.

"I told you I never wanted to see you again," she said. "And I meant it."

"Oh, come on Syd. I thought you'd have cooled off by now. I came down to escort you back. I thought you'd enjoy my company after all the time in this God forsaken jungle." He wiped sweat off his brow with his sleeve. "How can you stand it here in this humidity and with all these bugs?"

Sydney, aware of the others who were gathering for dinner, turned and walked out of the dining hall toward the hammock room. She didn't want to make a scene. Richard followed her.

"How did you find me?"

"It wasn't that difficult. I talked to your associates who said they didn't know where you went, but said you wanted to get as far away as you could. Being you come here so often, I concluded you'd be here and then verified it, and whalla, here I am." Richard seemed rather proud of his detective work and was delusional about Sydney's feelings. He truly thought she'd have changed her mind by now and would want him back in her life. After all, few could resist his charms, or so he thought.

Sydney stood directly in front of him with a stern look. "I told you it was over and I meant it, Richard. I don't love you. I don't want you in my life. I don't ever want to see you again. How much clearer can I make it? We're finished. We have been for a long time."

He ran his fingertips along her bare arm. "Aw, Syd. You know you don't mean it," he began.

Sydney forcefully brushed his hand away. She could tell he'd been drinking.

"I do mean it. Damn it, Richard. Are you so stuck on yourself that you can't accept rejection? Listen to me," she was almost shouting now. "I don't want you here. I don't want you anywhere near me!"

She could see the lines on his face harden. He roughly grabbed her arm to usher her into a more private space. "I just spent a fortune to travel almost two days, going through five airports, and a couple of freakin' scary boat rides to find you. And this is what I get? We need to talk," he insisted.

Sydney pulled away from him. "I never wanted you to come here. I'm sorry you wasted your time and money. We've been over and over this before and have nothing to talk about. Nothing has changed. Now, please, leave me alone. Just leave. Get out of my life."

Richard was getting angry now and reached for her again. Everything happened so quickly that Sydney wasn't really sure what had transpired. She remembered slapping Richard and then all of a sudden someone grabbed her from behind and pushed her into the shadows. The man confronted Richard and just as it was about to get physical, others appeared and soon Richard was ushered down the long walkway to the dock, cussing and swearing that it was all just a misunderstanding, that he was finished with the ungrateful bitch anyhow.

Sydney sighed some relief when she heard the boat heading down river. She was visibly shaken and a bit stunned that Richard had actually tracked her all the way down here. She only hoped that her message would sink in and his pride would keep him away from her. Forever.

She stepped out of the shadows and saw the outline of the man who had rescued her walking toward her. It couldn't be. Was she somehow transposing an image on someone else to indulge her longing for Drew? A character mirage? Had he really come for her? But when Drew looked up and she saw the disbelief on his face, her hopes were dashed. She knew he hadn't come to the lodge looking for her at all. He was just as surprised to see her. Him rescuing her was just a weird coincidence.

"Sydney?" he questioned his own eyes. "Sydney!" he repeated. "I didn't know it was you. Are you all right? Did he hurt you?"

"I'm OK," she replied. "Just a little stunned."

"Did you know this man?"

"I. . .I came here to get away from him. It was Richard. He just won't accept that our relationship is over. . .has been over for a long time. I can't believe he came here looking for me."

"I don't think he'll bother you anymore," Drew consoled. "Augusto and the others are taking him back to the main lodge and then directly to the Iquitos airport in the morning. He said he just wanted to get out of here and go back home where he was appreciated or something like that.

"Sydney. I can't believe you're here—at the lodge! Did you just arrive? I thought you went home. Where have you been?" Drew was full of questions. He was so happy to see her that he wanted to gather her into his arms and never let her go. At first he felt the same reaction in her, but then he sensed restraint. Was it because she was shaken by Richard's arrival in the jungle, or was she still angry with him because he had disrespected the shaman's abilities—because he suggested Juan would die in Rosita's care? After reading her journal entries he also realized that by doubting Rosita, he was insulting her, whether she had accepted her own role as a shaman or not.

"Can we go inside and talk?" he calmly suggested when she didn't answer his questions. He opened the wooden screen door and followed her through. They stood in the hammock room staring at each other for a few awkward moments, remembering their first meeting in the hammock room of the main lodge.

"I'm surprised you're still here," Sydney finally said. "I thought you had gone back to your hospital practice days ago."

"I was told that you left," he stated. "Why did Reagan . . . everyone. . .lie to me?"

"No one lied. I asked them to tell you I had left. I did. I left the lodge. I came here. I...I needed to be alone to sort things out," she hesitated, lowing her gaze to the floorboards.

"I thought you left because you never wanted to see me again," Drew finally said. "Sydney, I'm sorry I was so close minded in thinking I was the only one who could save the boy. I should have respected the native culture here and their medicine, at least given it a chance."

"I thought you would never want to see me after the things I said to you. I'm sorry, Drew. I understand better now why you're so driven to help people. I'm so sorry. . ." but before she could finish her sentence, Drew pulled her to him and kissed her, yielding to the raw passion they had the night of the storm. Sydney returned his kisses with the same fervor. Her body tingled all over. The fire was still there.

"Don't be sorry," he whispered, catching his breath. "Don't ever be sorry." Their emotions were so intense at that moment, that he wanted to make love to her right then and there, under the thatched conical roof of the hammock hut, but as his hands roamed her body, Sydney pulled away.

"No," she sighed, breathing heavily. "Not like this. We have a lot to talk through before we make commitments of any kind. I've gone through a lot of agony over you while you were gone and I need to sort through this."

Drew struggled to contain himself. He wouldn't let her go. "Don't you think I've gone through the same emotions? I want you, Sydney. I want you more than anything." He kissed her again, but could feel her resistance. He let loose his grip.

"OK. You're right. If anything is to become of. . .of us, we need to talk it through. I understand. I do. It's not just about lust and desire, Sydney. I know we have this intense sexual attraction for each other and it's wonderful. I can't get enough of you and, believe me, I've never been this aggressive before with a woman. You bring out the animal in me. But for me it really goes much deeper than just physical attraction." He wanted to tell her that he loved her, but couldn't stand the thought of her not loving him back. He was afraid this might just have been a sexual fling for her to get over her relationship with Richard. The rebound romance she had warned him about. Yes, they needed to talk.

The dining hall was empty when they returned, but the staff had thoughtfully left food on the buffet for them. There was no electricity at the lodge and lanterns glowed on the tables, setting a romantic scene to already heightened appetites. The couple filled their plates, sat across from each at the table, and averted their personal conversation by talking about Juan and his recovery. Drew told her about the studying he had been doing with Rosita and Maria and that's why he came to the ARC lodge, to talk with the scientists about their plant research. Sydney was impressed. She so loved this man. Could she ever allow her vulnerability to show and let him know? Could he ever love her back the way she needed to be loved? Unconditionally. Equally.

Finally, when dinner was finished, Drew reached across the table and took Sydney's hand. He looked directly into her eyes.

"I understand your hesitancy to plunge into a serious relationship, Sydney, I really do. We both have scars from our past that we need to work through. I want you to know that I'm willing to go slowly, if that helps. I want you in my life."

Sydney started to respond.

"Just hear me out," he cut her off. "I've thought about this a lot and I need to say it. I'll be heading back to the States and then soon on to another Doctors Without Borders mission. You'll be off on assignment somewhere in the world for days at a time. It's what we do. It wouldn't be a typical relationship. It may be weeks in between when we see each other, so making commitments could be difficult."

Sydney's heart began to sink.

"But. . ." Drew carefully chose his words. "What I do know, is that I want you in my life as much as possible, whenever possible. I'm not sure what that means for either of us right now. We can define it as we go along. That is, if you're willing to take a chance on an egotistical, close-minded doctor."

Tears swelled in Sydney's eyes. He wanted her. But she was confused. Was he asking her to be his lover? Just what did he want from her?

"I don't know. . ." she stammered, wanting to ask for clarification of his proposal.

"What I'm trying to say . . .is that I love you, Sydney Knight, as crazy as that may sound. I didn't ever think I'd feel this way again. I love you."

Sydney stared at him, her heart going out to his vulnerability. He loved her! That's all she had hoped for. But Drew took her hesitancy as a negative. He closed his eyes and threw his head back to hold in his emotions. How could he have been so wrong about her returning his feelings? He was about to turn away in embarrassment, when he felt Sydney's arms around him, pulling him close to her.

"I've been longing to hear those words," she sobbed. "I love you too, Drew. I love you." Her words were drowned out by his lips as they covered her mouth with emotion, an emotion deeper than lustful passion. It was an emotion of the heart.

"I did mean it, though," Drew said as he caught his breath. "I think we need to take it slower and get to know each other better. Our romance. . .our lovemaking. . .has been amazing, but we both know there's more to a relationship than sex. It looks like we have a lot to learn about each other and I want to know what makes you tick, Sydney. I want to know what's inside that pretty head of yours and how you think. You intrigue me with your passion for life and I want that to rub off on me. Maybe I can let loose of some of my staunch beliefs and lighten up a bit with your help."

"I love you just the way you are, Drew," she responded. "I like the idea of going slower, of courtship, getting to know each other's minds. It makes for a much healthier relationship."

Drew held her close. What now? What did "going slow" mean?

They looked into each other's eyes and smiled, knowing exactly "what now" meant.

They retreated to Sydney's hut and this time their lovemaking took on a different sentiment. They leisurely undressed each other, keeping eye contact, clothing dropping to the floor. Drew picked Sydney's naked body up into his arms, kissing her full, welcoming lips with yearning tenderness. Sydney's voluptuous breasts massaged against Drew's chest and her breath quickened. Drew gently laid her on the bed and their hands slowly caressed each other to take in every inch of each other's bodies. Their prolonged, stimulating touch gave way to lustful fondling and stroking that aroused each other's senses to the fullest. Drew's wet kisses followed the curves of Sydney's body, tasting the hot fire of her skin as his lips explored and met her sexual desires. She sensually moaned as he stimulated her in every way possible. Sydney rolled on top of him and massaging his tightened muscles, she let her hair lightly touch his chest, as she kissed his belly, her lips caressing his aroused, throbbing body.

No longer able to contain themselves, their electrified bodies entwined, moving to a rhythm of sexual pleasure, convulsing and sighing to the communion of their intimacy. The lustful passion they had felt before was still there, but with a tender consciousness of a love that aroused them to erotic heights that neither of them had experienced before.

The music of their lovemaking vibrating into the night became one with the sounds of the jungle. The ambience of the rainforest played a night symphony to them as darkness turned into light under the jungle moon.

Morning found them spent, in deep sleep. Content. Wrapped in each other's arms.

fifteen

SPIRIT ANIMALS

Drew and Sydney's time alone at the research center was just what they needed. Drew quickly forgave Reagan for not telling him that Sydney was still in the jungle. Everything had worked out better than he could have expected.

"Rosita has inquired if you and Dr. Drew would like to do a private shamanic healing with her tonight," Dolly reported to Sydney when they returned to the main lodge. "It's kind of her to offer. I could join you as an interpreter if you like."

"I would love that," Sydney immediately replied. "We'll have to ask Drew if he's interested."

"I've already asked him," Dolly smiled. "He said he would be honored. So, right after dinner we'll have Ricardo take us to the village. Rosita is getting old and offered to do this in her home, rather than come here at night."

The single beam of a flashlight occasionally flashed on, watching for debris or swimming animals, as the lodge boat made its way toward Chino Village. Sydney had once asked why they didn't keep the light on for the entire trip when the boats traveled at night, instead of turning it on and off. The answer was logical.

"We only use the light if we think we see something foreign in the water. If we keep the light on," she was told, "our eyes only see what is in the path of its beam. But if we don't use the flashlight, our eyes adapt to the landscape of the water and riverbanks. We are like the animals of the jungle, tuned into the light of the stars and the moon to guide our way."

They arrived at their destination and as Ricardo docked the boat, Dolly led them up a series of wooden steps to the path that lead through the jungle to Rosita's stilted hut. She greeted them and motioned for them to sit on the wooden floor, anxious to begin her ceremony. The scene was similar to when she performed the ritual on Juan. She mixed her brew of chuchuhasi and passed it around twice for them to drink. She softly sang her beautiful chants, asking the Spirits to come through her and give her wisdom for this ritual. She smoked hand-rolled cigarettes of black tobacco, while looking up into the rafters, communing with her guides.

Then she moved over to Sydney and shook the shapaca leaves over her while she sang and blew smoke all around her. As she shook her fan of leaves, she lingered at Sydney's heart, shaking the leafy rattle extra hard and using her other hand to make a sort of clearing motion. She knowingly touched her hand to her own heart and, nodding her head, she smiled at Sydney.

She moved to Sydney's ankle and worked her rattle and smoke on the sprain Sydney had gotten during the flood. Drew watched intensely, knowing that Rosita had no prior knowledge of Sydney's injury. Surrounding the limb with smoke and shaking the shapaca leaves, the shaman concentrated on the exact area of the sprain, singing her healing prayers. She looked at Sydney as if to acknowledge the wound. Sydney nodded, responding to her discovery. Rosita made motions with her rattle as she was chasing the bad energy away from the ankle and sending in healing energy. She blew puffs of smoke around the entire area and then made three circles with her shapaca rattle over Sydney. Cupping her hands on the top of Sydney's head, Rosita blew through her fingers, releasing the spirit of a power animal into Sydney's body. She spoke to her in Spanish. Dolly translated.

"She says you have the strong spirit of a black panther protecting you here tonight. It's one of your spirit animals."

Sydney nodded in acceptance. She was familiar with the panther as one of her power animals.

Then the shaman moved to Drew. Repeating the leaf shaking and smoke blowing, she also spent extra time in the area of his heart, sending healing energy to any wounds he may have had lingering there. She continued to shake her magic around his body, but when she got to his throat, she put extra emphasis into her ritual. She moved her hand in a motion, beginning at the center of his chest up through his mouth, repeating this several times, following her motion with wisps of smoke from her cigarette. She placed her hand directly on the base of his throat, over his esophagus, and let it rest there. Drew could feel the heat of her hand penetrate through his shirt into his body. He swallowed hard and involuntarily belched out a loud burp. He was embarrassed and apologized. Rosita smiled.

She repeated the ritual of blowing a power animal into the top of Drew's head until her work was completed. With Dolly translating, she told Drew that he has the medicine of the snake connected to him as his spirit animal.

"A snake?" Drew whispered, as if he had heard her wrong. He had expected something big and courageous. After all, Sydney got a panther!

"A snake," Dolly repeated.

Rosita returned to her circle of healing tools and sat down. She spoke to Dolly, who translated.

"Rosita said that the Spirits she worked with tonight were laughing and dancing behind you. They were happy to be here in your healing and want you to know they will watch over you, if you so choose. She asked if you have any questions."

Drew was full of them.

"Ah. . . yes. First of all, thank you for honoring us with your healing and your wisdom," he began with complete respect. He had come a long way since Rosita's healing ceremony with Juan, when he watched from the shadows. Sydney was impressed.

"I don't know what it means to have a snake for a spirit animal. What is a spirit or power animal?"

Dolly again translated in terms Drew could understand.

"In shamanic belief every thing is alive and carries power and wisdom. Animal spirits are present with each individual, adding to their energy and protecting them from illness, similar to a guardian angel. Each spirit animal you have increases your power so that illnesses or negative energy can't enter your body. The Spirit also shares its natural instinctive wisdom with you."

Rosita continued, directing her words toward Drew.

Dolly explained. "She said the snake spirit is powerfully connected to life force and vital energy. When the snake spirit appears, it means that healing opportunities, important transitions and increased energy are manifesting. The presence of the snake in your life means you're in a time of change and it's there to guide you in your personal and spiritual growth."

Drew was surprised. He had always thought of the snake as a negative force.

Rosita read his thoughts and said, "To have a snake as a spirit animal is good. Spirit snakes appear when you're facing the unknown and need support to go forward. They remind you to stay grounded as you move through changes."

Dolly added, "Rosita said the snake is one of her power animals also. It's a common totem of healers."

Of course, Drew thought. The Caduceus. The medical symbol with the winged staff of Hermes entwined with two snakes. In Greek mythology, Hermes was a messenger between the gods and humans, which explains the wings, and a guide to the underworld, represented by the staff. The Greeks regarded snakes as sacred and used them in healing rituals. Snake venom was thought to be remedial and their skin-shedding was a symbol of rebirth and renewal. It made sense that his spirit animal would be a snake.

Drew smiled and looked at Rosita. She nodded with approval.

Dolly added some of her own wisdom, further explaining the importance of the local culture's beliefs around these totems or spirit animals.

"It's believed in many native cultures, that everyone has more than one guardian power animal or else the individual couldn't survive childhood. Over the course of life the person may have several. If one power animal leaves and another doesn't come to take its place, the person is considered to be disempowered and vulnerable to illness and even bad luck."

"So, what's the meaning of the black panther for Sydney?" Drew was curious. Sydney had been sitting silently during the discussion, enjoying Drew's interaction with the mysteries of the Spirit world.

Rosita spoke through Dolly's interpretation.

"She said that Sydney is blessed with a fierce guardian, that a panther spirit animal is powerful and protective. It symbolizes courage, valor and power."

Rosita continued, looking into Sydney's eyes to be sure she was listening. She used her hands to accent her words.

"The black panther is a symbol of feminine energy, of the mother, the dark moon and the power of the night. She encourages you to understand the power within the shadows, accept it, eliminate any fear of the unknown, and reclaim your strength."

Sydney knew the big cat was one of her power animals. She had been told that by other shaman in different parts of the world, and by Rosita years ago. But hearing Rosita's translation now, had deeper meaning to her. *". . . understand the power within the shadows and accept these powers."* Those were commanding words, knowing what Sydney did about shamanism and how it has affected her throughout her life.

Dolly interjected, "I know people with this animal totem who are highly intuitive and artistic. When a panther appears, it's time to release your passions, live your dreams and begin a new chapter in your life knowing you're guided and protected. Does that ring a bell with you, Syd?"

Sydney nodded, looking toward the floorboards. Somehow, in the mix of relationships in her life, Sydney had gotten separated from her spirit animal. She had forgotten to use that intuition and voice that steered her in the right direction. . .the voice of this powerful guardian. She had to come back to the jungle where the black panther lived to draw from its energy and guidance. She needed to allow the Spirit of this animal to reside within her again, to carry its energy with her as she stepped out of the shadow into her dreams of a positive, happy relationship and eventually to accept her own powers as a healer.

It was getting late and Sydney thanked Rosita with a gift of black tobacco cigarettes she had purchased earlier in the market in Iquitos. She knew it was Rosita's favorite gift, and a necessary tool for her work that was only obtained through the generosity of those who traveled to the city for supplies. As they parted, Rosita hugged both Sydney and Drew, sending warm energy through them that only a shaman possessed—energy that was translated into pure love, acceptance, and respect of a fellow healer. Dolly, likewise, hugged this old friend of hers and thanked her for the visit.

The boat ride back to the lodge brought silence while Sydney and Drew digested what had transpired with Rosita's shamanic healing. A thousand stars shone above, guiding the way for Ricardo's keen eyes to maneuver the boat up river.

They thanked Dolly and Ricardo and said goodnight as soon as they reached the lodge. They went to Sydney's room and sat on the bed. Both were in a pensive state of mind.

"How's your ankle?" Drew asked.

"Pain free," Sydney smiled.

"That was pretty amazing. Watching the shaman work on your ankle was a real eye-opener. She couldn't have known you had the injury. Those are some pretty powerful Spirits working with her."

"Yes, they are," Sydney agreed. "I also noticed that she spent a lot of time working on your neck or chest. Are you having some trouble that you'd like to share?"

Drew was hesitant. "It's not a big deal," he finally said. "I have a hiatal hernia which causes Gastroesophageal—acid reflux. I take meds for it. I'm going in to have minor surgery when I return home, to open the narrowing of my esophagus. It's hereditary, but I'm sure stress at work adds to it."

"What are your symptoms?" Sydney asked.

"Now you sound like the doctor," he said, not liking talking about his ailments, but knowing she wouldn't stop asking questions until he replied.

"It varies. If I don't take my medication I can feel a spell coming on with heartburn, the hiccups, and I start to burp a lot. Before I started meds, I often had earaches, hoarseness, a dry cough and sinus problems. It was pretty easy to diagnose. Now I try to avoid citrus and juices, fatty foods, coffee, black tea, carbonated drinks, and things like chocolate, onions, peppermint, spicy foods. . .pretty sad, huh?"

"Especially no coffee and chocolate," Sydney laughed. "Are there foods that help?" She was curious.

"You probably saw me eating a lot of bananas while I've been here and drinking chamomile tea. Things like apple cider vinegar, fresh ginger, turmeric, and aloe vera juice help. It's hard to use some of these things, though, when I'm traveling."

He shifted his thoughts.

"It was really weird the way I belched when Rosita was working on me. I felt like this huge blockage was just coming out of me in that one billow of air. It was as if she was actually clearing away the hernia and opening my throat."

"Don't be surprised when you get back home if your doctor says you don't need the surgery. . .that your hiatal hernia is gone, along with your acid reflux," Sydney said.

"That would be a miracle," Drew responded. A week ago he wouldn't even have considered the thought. Now, he would be anxious to see when he got back what his diagnosis would be. Deep down, he hoped Rosita had healed him, but he wasn't ready to go so far as to admit that quite yet.

"How about you? Anything the doctor should know about?"

"Nope. I'm pretty healthy. . .thanks to my regular visits to Rosita and her healing Spirits."

Drew looked at Sydney pensively. "You know, a week or so ago, my scientific mind wouldn't have believed any of this was possible, but now. . .now, I believe that anything could be possible."

That night Drew and Sydney lay side-by-side, under the mosquito netting of Sydney's bed and they just held each other. Their heads swam with visions of Rosita singing and chanting her healing energy into them. Images of black panthers and snakes moved through their thoughts as they followed the power and wisdom of these spirit animals into their dreams.

~ sixteen ~

BEGINNINGS

The next day thoughts of what the future would hold was heavy on their minds. Not only in terms of what they had learned about themselves or about the power that each of them held within and how that related to their responsibilities and intentions, but also about their lives together. Their time in the jungle was nearing an end and they both wondered how returning home, returning to reality, would define their relationship. It would be easy to say that love overruled career, but they were both realistic and knew that their jobs also had an important role in the lives of others. They would have to manage to steal as much time together as they could. That would take commitment.

Reagan flew home a few days earlier than Drew, but before he left he and Drew had a long, serious conversation.

"I have to admit," Drew said, "that I'm so inspired by the hard working jungle clinicians and shamans, that I think I've decided to leave the hospital. I'll give them plenty of notice, of course, that is if I even still have a job when I return. I'm going to go back to school—for a graduate study of tropical medicine. I'd like to blend my skills as a doctor with a scientific career investigating tropical diseases and cures."

Reagan wasn't surprised. He knew how unhappy his friend had been in mainstream medicine. It wasn't the work he was doing, rather it was the bureaucracy that went with the job. He didn't like all the paperwork and rules. He just wanted to help people, like they had been doing while in the jungle.

"I've been thinking about this a lot," Drew continued. "To complement the university scientific training I'll be getting, I'd like to make regular visits to the Tahuayo in order to learn more from the native clinicians, as well as the local shamans."

"Wow. You've come a long way from the Dr. Drew I knew when we left the States," Reagan commented. "But, knowing you the way I do, I think it's a good choice and you'll be a lot happier for it, just as long as you drag me with you whenever you come down here. It's been a profound experience for me as well."

"Will do. It's been quite a humbling experience, I think, for both of us."

Reagan proposed that they could also contact their network of medical teams, doctors, nurses, dentists, assistants who may also want to volunteer at the clinic and to experience the jungle adventure the Tahuayo Amazon Lodge had to offer.

Realizing how important it was to implement alternative and traditional medicine, they would see if it were possible to set up a program that would include Rosita, Maria, and other shaman and herbalist and healers in the area to teach natural medicinal choices and share their wisdom with the medical teams who came, expanding their insights into the world of rain forest remedies. This would bring Reagan and Drew back to the jungle as often as possible.

Dolly was excited about this possibility and insisted that since Sydney had a history of leading groups to the jungle, she could oversee travel arrangements and assist guests. It was a win win situation. Deep down, although they never told Sydney that Drew had read her journal, both Dolly and Drew hoped that it would also spur Sydney to eventually accept her role as a healer and she'd begin to use her own gifts in whatever ways she was meant.

The nature of Sydney and Drew's careers would allow time for several of these trips a year and that would be wonderful, Drew thought, but he lamented at the time in between. They both lived in New York, but were hundreds of miles apart. Phone, email, texting—it wasn't the same as physically being together.

"We'll make it happen somehow," he assured Sydney when they discussed their options. They held each other close, filled with a mix of emotions —happiness, gratitude, tenderness, adoration, desire, love and sadness.

But now it was time to make the journey back to Iquitos.

"Goodbye Dolly," Sydney hugged her friend, the jungle's daughter. "I'll miss you. Thank you for everything and for being my personal counselor!"

"You'll be back soon," Dolly said with confidence, squeezing her hand. "The jungle has a way of calling you here for many reasons."

Dolly gave Drew a hug. "I'm so happy for the two of you. You deserve each other. Greet your friend Reagan when you get back to the States. We have a lot of organizing to do to prepare our project of teaching your medical experts the healing ways of the jungle. We'll be in touch soon."

The couple said their goodbyes to the Bichina, Rolex, Augusto, Ricardo and the other jungle lodge staff while Arturo helped them board the boat for the long ride back to Iquitos. They savored every moment of the boat trip, soaking in the sunshine, the beauty of the birds and wildlife along the river, the tall, straight trees reaching into the jungle canopy, exotic flowers, and everyday life along the Amazon, as they said goodbye to the jungle.

They would fly from Iquitos to Lima before their flight to the States, and had arranged for a few days in Lima together to enjoy the cultural museums, shop the artisan markets and to have more intimate time, making every moment count. They were on the same flight back to New York, but each knew that parting would be difficult. After all they had shared on their jungle adventure, how could either of them go back to the reality of life as they knew it.

"I have one request," Sydney said to Drew before they boarded their flight.

"Just one?" Drew teased.

"Will you write to me? I don't mean emails or texts. I mean old fashioned letters. I want to see your handwriting and feel the words you're writing. It's so much more personal. Will you do that?"

"Only if you write back," he said. "I suppose I'll have to work on my doctor's penmanship. It wouldn't do any good if you couldn't read my handwriting." He smiled, thinking of little gifts he could tuck into his letters, mementos of his love for her or simple things that made him think of her—a feather, a poem, pieces of plants or herbs he learned about in the jungle. Yes, this would be nice.

"And you'll have to put drops of your perfume on every page, so I can inhale the scent of you from afar," he said. Sydney smiled at his romantic nature. How she loved this man.

As they snuggled close to each other on the airplane, heading back to their commitments, Sydney was reminded of a flight not so long ago when she watched newlyweds in row 13 who, lost in their love, couldn't take their hands off each other. Now she knew how they felt. She understood that uninhibited desire that comes with true love. The love of a soulmate.

Neither wanted to face the real world, yet knew they had responsibilities they needed to return to. They vowed to see each other as often as they could and to talk every day. Love would ensure their rendezvous.

They lingered in each other's arms at JFK, clinging to their dreams and memories of making love deep in the jungle, surrounded by the sounds of nature and a thousand stars overhead.

"I'm going to miss the smell of your hair," Drew said, nestling his face into her thick blonde mane. "And the touch of your soft skin." He lightly ran his fingertips along her neck, sending electricity through her.

"And how about my fine mind and quirky sense of humor?" she playfully questioned.

"Well, that too," he quickly admitted. "I'm going to miss everything about you. Every part of you." He kissed her again and then reached into his bag and retrieved a tissue-wrapped gift.

"A little something for you," he said, handing it to her.

"Really?" Sydney was surprised. "I didn't expect anything."

"Let's just say that sometimes the things you least expect might just be the things you need the most."

Wondering what he meant, Sydney carefully removed the soft yellow tissue wrapping to reveal a beautiful flower. . .a large, bold bird-of-paradise.

"My favorite flower!" she exclaimed. "How did you know?"

"Intuition," he said, but before Sydney could reflect further, he enfolded her in a tender embrace. "I just knew," he whispered.

"Oh, one more thing," he said as he quickly pulled out his cell phone and turned it back on. He put his arm around Sydney and took a selfie of the two of them. . .and her bird of paradise flower. . .one last memory of their jungle adventure.

"I'll text it to you," he promised, putting the phone back into his pocket.

Sydney laughed. She had plenty of photos of them together and separately from the trip, but

Drew hadn't seen most of them. They'd been too busy. A selfie. Yes, they were indeed back to reality.

Now, they stood in the airport, holding each other, lost in time, wanting this moment to last before Drew made his way to the train station and headed north a couple of hours to the Catskills and Sydney hailed a taxi to transport her through the concrete jungle to Manhattan.

Along with finding love in the Amazon, Sydney and Drew had each healed old emotional scars. That was a big step in nurturing a healthy relationship. Both knew their lives would never be the same.

And every night they would be together in their burning dreams, thirsting for each other, entwined in love, forever joined under the soft, yellow glow of the jungle moon.

Jungle Moon ~ 222 ~ Connie Bickman

ABOUT THE AUTHOR

Author Connie Bickman draws her writing inspiration from a long newspaper career, international travels to more than 40 developing countries as a photojournalist, occasional travel guide journeys, along with a love of detail, native beliefs and traditional history, to provide background for her Sydney Knight adventure novels. Watch for more books in this series in the near future that will include some of the author's own travel escapades woven into the life of Sydney Knight.

After living in Minnesota for much of her life, Connie lived a few years in Woodstock, NY, and is currently settling her gypsy bones to write and photograph in Arizona.

www.conniebickman.com

64917926R00135

Made in the USA
Lexington, KY
25 June 2017